Portals

A Sable BooKnight Anthology

Cover designed by GetCovers.

The names in this story are fictitious. Any similarities are strictly coincidental.

Book ISBN 978-1-990282-40-9

eBook ISBN 978-1-990282-41-6

A Sable BooKnight Anthology

Contents

A Waltz in Time

Sianyn Leigh

Aimee Thalmann set a glazed yeast donut with a napkin on the counter at the Birch Park Retirement Home reception desk. A box containing 2 dozen more balanced in one hand, she leaned over the counter with a smile brighter than anyone had a right to at 6:30 am.

"Morning, Suzy. I'm here to see Evelyn."

Suzy smiled at the younger woman, the hard lines around her mouth a clear indication genuine joy was a strain so early in the morning. Gently lifting the sugary bribe from the counter, Suzy jerked her head towards the hall.

"Morning, Aimee. Go on in. She's in the dining room already."

"Thanks, Suzy."

The rising sun peeked in the cafeteria windows, glinting off polished tables and basking the room in a warm glow. Residents were slowly trickling in, a shuffling parade of walkers, wheelchairs, and slippered feet. Aimee headed straight for the table just inside the doorway and set down the box of donuts, chestnut curls bouncing on her shoulder.

"Hey, Jan, how's everything going this morning?" Aimee greeted, keeping her tone cheerful.

Jan, the nursing aide usually assigned to breakfast duty, pulled the box closer with a grateful sigh, flipping open the lid to pull out a doughy pick-me-up. The elderly man in the chair next to her watched with greedy eyes as she bit into the fluffy ring, pushing his spoon back and forth in the bowl of unsweetened oatmeal with a distinct lack of enthusiasm.

"So good," Jan moaned around a mouthful. Swallowing, she continued, "Evie's in her usual corner. She's been feeling down lately. Her daughter still hasn't come to see her."

"Still? It's been months."

Jan shrugged. "You see it all the time. Some people aren't willing to forgive their childhood, and this is a good place to set Mom down and forget about her." Jan reached for another donut. "You're so nice to sit with her, Aimee. She really looks forward to your talks."

Aimee tossed her a smile and turned towards the far corner. She looked forward to her talks with Evelyn, too, but not for any sentimental reasons. She'd only met the elder woman six months ago during an interview for a news article–a simple fluff piece about holiday activities in retirement homes. Most residents offered cute, heartwarming accounts of craft activities with the grandkids or holiday-themed bingo nights. But when it was Evelyn's turn, Aimee knew she had a *real* story.

"Hi, Miss Evie, how are you doing today?" Aimee asked, sliding into the chair next to the older woman.

Evelyn Nichols had once been an elegant woman. Whispers of that former poise still shone through in the patrician features, the high swoop of her white hair, and the embroidered dressing gown draped over the ruffled, baby pink nightdress. Every time Aimee saw her, Evie was dressed in vintage, like she'd just stepped out of a *Bewitched* episode.

"They don't believe me. They never believe me," Evelyn muttered, picking at a loose thread on her robe. A plate of egg whites and grits sat forgotten on the table next to a small glass of cranberry juice. She swiveled her head to Aimee, setting red-rimmed, watery eyes on the young journalist. "But you believe me, don't you, Andy?"

"It's Aimee, Miss Evie. Andy's your grandson. He couldn't come today," Aimee explained carefully, keeping her tone even. The nurses warned her to be gentle when Evie had *one of those days*, when time and people became a big jumble and she couldn't remember if it was 2005 or 1985.

"Names," Evelyn moaned, shaking her head. "So many names. Too many names."

Her agitation rose in time with her voice, culminating in the thunk of her fragile, balled fist on the table. Aimee wrapped her hands around Evelyn's thinner one, glancing over her shoulder to make sure no one had noticed.

“It’s okay, Evelyn, it’s okay,” Aimee promised. “We’re not going to talk about names today. Let’s talk about dancing.”

“Dancing?” Evelyn asked, her face relaxing as her hand unclenched.

Aimee extricated one of her hands to pull her voice recorder out of her pocket and lay it on the table in front of Evelyn, the red light blinking in readiness. “Yes, dancing,” she repeated. “Tell me about that time you went dancing.”

“I shouldn’t have gone, of course,” Evelyn began, turning her head to look out the window wistfully. “I still had a baby at home, and my Charlie was working nights at the factory back then. But he said I deserved a night of fun. So, I went. My friend Lisa drove …”

Aimee pulled up in front of the old theater and shut off the engine, leaning over to peek up at the marquee. Havermore Theater had been the jewel of downtown back in its heyday but had fallen into neglect in the fifty years since. Bricks crumbled at the corners, and wood warped under sun-bleached paint. The lobby that once burst with movie-goers every premiere now barely saw more than a couple dozen on a good night. Repurposed as a budget theater, it now only showed movies six months out of date three nights a week, plus one matinee on Sunday.

Since the 50s, the upstairs room had doubled as a ballroom space for parties. Evelyn Nichols had gone to a party there in 1966, leaving her infant daughter at home with her husband, and didn’t come back for ten years. On her mysterious return, her abandoned family asked where she had been, but Evelyn insisted she'd only been dancing.

It happened again in the winter of 1978. Evelyn went to see a matinee and didn't return for a full decade. By then, her husband had been killed in a factory accident, and her daughter was married with a family of her own, unwilling to have a relationship with a mother who had walked away not once, but twice. In all that time, Evelyn never changed her story: she'd only been dancing.

That's what had attracted Aimee to the case. Everyone discounted Evelyn as unstable and addled, but Aimee made people's stories her career. She knew an untruth when she heard one. Evelyn was telling–or, at least, believed she was telling–the truth, and that had piqued Aimee's interest.

After that first interview, she'd dug into the story and found not only the articles about Evelyn's disappearance and miraculous return, but other disappearances related to the theater. Evelyn hadn't been the only one to return, either. A teen went to a party in the upstairs room in 1984 and returned in 1994 with no recollection of the missing years. Similar stories had occurred in 1958, 1972, and 1987, all reports of missing persons who went into the theater only to re-emerge exactly ten years later. Each account was dismissed as amnesia, runaways, or mental health episodes. If anyone had bothered to cross-reference the instances, they would have seen every returning person told a variation of the same story: they'd been at a party the whole time.

Popping fresh batteries in her camera, Aimee looped it over her neck. Taking a deep breath, she exited the car and knocked on the heavy glass door of the theater. It was usually closed on Tuesdays, but the owner had been more than happy to open on his day off for a chance to get some free press in the local paper.

The owner, a man named Paul Finch, unlocked the door at her approach.

"Hi, you must be Aimee," he greeted, holding the door open to let her inside. Thin, greying hair brushed the collar of his faded blue polo. Deep laugh lines creased his face, and a pair of thick glasses pushed divots into the bridge of his nose. He looked exactly as Aimee expected an aging film buff who spent all his time serving burnt popcorn would look.

"Yes, thank you so much for doing this today. I really appreciate it," Aimee greeted, shaking his hand once he let go of the door.

"No problem, happy to help." Paul shoved his hands in the pockets of his jeans and gestured to the stairs with a jerk of his head. "The ballroom is just up there. I left all the doors unlocked. Feel free to look around. I'll be in the office if you need anything."

Aimee thanked him again while heading up the stairs, as he disappeared through the door behind the concession stand. The ballroom, used as storage for the past decade, still held some of its former glory. Ornate woodwork; mirror-paneled walls; burnished chandeliers hung with sparkling crystals. Time had darkened the metal, and several of the crystals were missing, but Aimee could well imagine their brilliance in decades past. Now, instead of colorful party dresses and champagne glasses, the dim bulbs illuminated discarded theater chairs and broken concession equipment.

Aimee stood amidst the maze of stacked chairs and leaning boxes, unsure what she was looking for. Slipping the voice recorder from her pocket, she hit the play button. Evelyn's weak, thready voice echoed off the high ceiling.

"I wasn't looking for the door. I think the door was looking for me. It found me down the side hall. I thought it was the powder room, but it was a whole other world." *click*

The side hall. Aimee scanned the room, peering around stacks until she caught a glimpse of deep shadows behind a sun-faded curtain. Her heart raced as she stepped over and yanked the curtain aside. Two doors sat recessed into the damask wallpaper, facing each other. Her pulse quickened even more, and her hand trembled as she slid the voice recorder back in her pocket. Holding the camera up, she flipped open the viewfinder and hit record, pointing it down the hallway.

"Here I am in the upstairs ballroom of the Havermore Theater, where Evelyn and several other people went missing in cases spanning decades. According to Evelyn's testimony, she went through a door in this hallway into another ballroom. When she came out again, ten years had passed."

Keeping her camera trained on the door to the right first, Aimee crept down the hall as she spoke. "According to city records, the building blueprints do not show a second ballroom, but Evelyn was not the only person to claim another room exists."

She paused in front of the door and reached out to grasp the knob. Taking a deep breath, she twisted and pushed. The door swung open, revealing a darkened but completely unremarkable restroom.

The tension left Aimee's shoulders in a deflated huff. Flicking on the light just inside the door, Aimee panned the camera over the row of sinks and stalls.

"Definitely no parties going on in here," she mumbled to the mic, switching the light off and backing out of the room.

With a quick turn, she faced the camera to the door directly across from the first. "Let's see what's behind door number two."

She swung the door open only to find another restroom. She groaned. Aimee didn't really believe in the supernatural or magic or even time loops, but a story like this would have propelled her career straight into viral journalist status. Her paycheck could really have used the boost. And it would have been nice to prove Evelyn and the others had been telling the truth.

"There you have it, folks," Aimee said, closing the restroom door. "Just another hoax to hide bad decisions and family secrets."

She let the camera drop to the end of the tether, catching a glint out of the corner of her eye as she pivoted to leave. Squinting in the half-light filtering in from the ballroom windows, she looked for the source of the flash. The sun reflecting off a polished handle flashed again, and Aimee did a double take. A door sat at the back of the hall, more ornate than the restroom doors, with lattice carved into the facade and an intricate brass plate around the curving handle. She could swear the door hadn't been there a moment ago.

Aimee reversed the recording several minutes and played it back. That door definitely hadn't been there a moment ago. It wasn't a play of shadows or the angle of the light. The video clearly showed nothing but a smooth wall where now there stood a gleaming door.

A shiver moved over her skin in a wave, the hairs on her arms rising to attention. Evelyn's words swirled in her head: *the door was looking for me*. Aiming her camera in front of her again, Aimee slowly stepped towards the door, not daring to blink lest it wink out of existence again. The air around her seemed to grow more electric with each step closer.

The thought of leaving flickered through her mind. Evelyn lost twenty years of her life from this door, did Aimee want to risk the same? Yet, how could she pass up the chance to find out exactly what happened to so many people? To prove something *inexplicable* happened–a time warp, a pocket dimension, whatever–that it wasn't a hoax and the extraordinary does exist, would catapult her career into the stratosphere. She couldn't pass up a chance like that.

Just some video, that's all she wanted. Prove the room exists. No need to go inside. Just film whatever she could from the hall, then leave and maybe interview more witnesses.

The brightly polished handle was in arm's reach now. Taking a deep, steadying breath, Aimee reached out and pushed down on the lever, letting the door swing open. A wave of perfumed air rolled over her as twinkling light and orchestral music spilled from the doorway. Laid out inside was a glittering, luxurious ballroom, complete with mirrored walls, opulent chandeliers, and silken draperies. Aimee could see waltzing couples twirling across the floor, dressed in flowing gowns and embroidered suits out of time with current fashion by at least two hundred years. A sideboard stretched along the inner wall, laden with hors d'oeuvres and champagne glasses.

It was everything Evelyn had described, like something straight out of a Charles Perrault tale, dazzling and wondrous and completely magical. Still, Aimee was unprepared for the awe that washed over her. She wanted to turn away, to take her video evidence and break the story for the world, to prove Evelyn had never abandoned her family on purpose. Yet she couldn't make her feet turn around. Something begged her to look closer, to go inside, to dance and experience what Evelyn had felt during her endless waltz.

Taking a hesitant step forward, Aimee crossed over the threshold. The air snapped around her with a pop, like she'd descended from a high altitude. The music halted as the dancers froze, turning elegantly coiffed heads in her direction. Her stomach dropped under the scrutiny. The camera slipped from her grasp, saved by the strap around her neck. She swiveled on her heel, ready to jump right back through the door, but it was gone. Nothing but blue damask wallpaper and tasseled drapes where the door had been just seconds ago.

"Welcome, my dear. I do so love to see new faces."

Aimee spun back around at the sound of the lyrical, deep voice behind her. One dancer had stepped forward, a man in a blue velvet jacket with shining silver embroidery. Blonde curls tumbled around a strikingly sharp and highlighted face. Bright pink blush slashed under his high cheekbones, making them look sharp enough to cut, his eyes outlined in black and lips glowing with crimson gloss. It was a look that screamed high fashion or cabaret, yet managed to look ethereal rather than feminine.

His eyes glanced up and down her body, and his lips twisted up in a half smile that said he liked what he saw. His voice deepened ever so slightly, taking on a coquettish tone as he continued, "I do hope you'll stay a while."

"Hi. I, uh, didn't mean to crash the party," Aimee stumbled. She'd faced her share of flirtatious men before, but none that looked this gorgeous. Her whole reason for even being in the room evaporated under his attention. Whatever she forgot, it was worth it just for that smile.

"Think nothing of it," he replied with a delicate wave of his hand. "This party is for ... anyone." He paused, letting his intense gaze rest on her long enough for her cheeks to blush. Taking a step forward, he reached his hand out to her. "Care for a dance?"

Clamping down on her bottom lip against the heat his stare generated, Aimee accepted his hand and allowed herself to be pulled onto the dance floor. The coldness of his skin surprised her as he slid an arm around her back and drew her close, a shiver traveling across her shoulders as she realized the whole room was just as cold. She wished she'd bothered to grab a sweater before heading to the party.

Aimee looked down at herself, wondering why she wore jeans and a tee shirt when everyone else dressed to impress in sparkling finery. It felt rude to be the only one dressed so casually. Why didn't she wear something nice? Whose party was this, anyway?

"You seem very far away. A minute for your thoughts?"

The odd turn of phrase drew Aimee's attention back to her dance partner. He looked down at her with an elegant, interested smile, and Aimee was struck once again by how otherworldly the man was. His manners, his poise, his exquisitely beautiful face–all looked human, but something wasn't quite right.

It was the eyes. Despite the kind tone, earnest expression, and graceful sway, none of it reflected in the cold, glass-like shine of his eyes. Uneasiness filled her.

"I'm sorry, I just realized I haven't paid my respects to the host."

She tried to pull away, but the man held fast. She gave him a polite smile, wondering if an "accidental" tread on the toes would loosen his grip.

"We are the Host, darling," he said, gesturing to the other guests with a thrust of his chin. "You can pay me, if you like. An hour for a twirl. A month for a waltz. An eternity for a kiss."

He hissed the last syllable, turning the almost playful remark into something bordering on sinister. Aimee fought the urge to recoil, hiding her discomfort with a polite chuckle. She didn't understand where her reluctance came from. He was charming, attractive, engaging. Yet, every fiber of her being screamed to run before she ran out of time.

"An eternity for a kiss? Seems a bit steep for something so small," Aimee returned, struggling to keep her tone light. She needed time to think, to distract him until she could slip away.

His laugh echoed off the mirrored walls like cracking crystal. "Oh, my dear, you will find it is time well spent, I dare say. *They* certainly didn't mind the price."

Aimee followed his nod to a trio of guests seated on a bench on the far side of the room. Two women and a man, all well into their elder years and looking even less party-appropriate than Aimee. The man wore classic 70s bellbottoms and a crocheted vest, his long grey hair hanging well past his shoulders, long legs stretched out and chin tucked down. The smaller woman wore a blue pinafore, white curls tied up in matching ribbon, upper body half-propped up against the other woman slouched in a beige 1920s day dress. All three had swollen, painful-looking sores marring the soles of their bare feet, as if they had been shoeless for a very long time. They were distressingly thin, bones starkly outlined at the joints and their skin slightly ashen and loose.

They looked half-starved and in dire need of medical help. She couldn't believe no one had bothered to do anything yet. Aimee's heart twisted, and she took a half-step towards them. But again, the man tightened his grip and kept her at his side.

"Let me go," she demanded, yanking her arm against his grasp. His fingers remained wrapped around her wrist like a vise. "They need help."

He scoffed. "They are spent. No time left. Ignore them and they'll fade away, eventually."

"That's ridiculous. How can you just leave them there?"

The silk-clad shoulders rose and fell in a delicate shrug. "Their dance is over, but the night goes on. Yours will end soon enough, if you wish to join them. But for now, waltz with me."

The man adjusted his hand so their palms touched once more, the hand at her back a cold weight. Snapping back the retort she desperately wanted to voice, Aimee fell into the rhythm of the waltz, taking his lead. Her mind swirled in a dance of its own, searching every angle for a way out of the situation. She just wanted to get home, out of his reach, out of this ballroom.

She glanced around the room as they twirled. No doors, no windows. Sure, there were drapes and tapestries, but they framed only blank sections of wall. How did she get in here, wherever *here* was? Why couldn't she remember?

The man leaned in close as if going for a kiss, and Aimee leaned her head back to keep her lips out of his reach. Closing his eyes, he breathed in deep, moving his head back and forth slightly, smelling her. Aimee's stomach fluttered. Her attraction to his exquisite features and alluring tone warred with the instinct of impending danger.

"You smell like a New Day," he said, tightening his arm around her waist.

Something hard dug into her chest, and Aimee looked down. The camera still hung from her neck. She only used this camera for work. That meant she was here on a job. What had she been working on?

Something deep in the back of her brain sparked to life. Evelyn. She was here because of Evelyn and all the other people who had gone missing in the upstairs ballroom.

"What is this place? Who are you?" Aimee demanded, piecing it all back together. Missing time. Endless parties. Disappearing rooms. She wasn't in her own reality anymore.

His answer confirmed her suspicions. "This is the Light Court, of course. Land of Everlasting Youth, Hall of the Faerie Host."

Stories of the Fae Folk had been bandied about for centuries, but that's all anyone ever thought of them: stories. How could it possibly be true? Immortal beings. Magical realms. Enchantments. It was all a bunch of superstitious nonsense born of folklore and misunderstood science. But then, how could dozens of people disappear for decades only to reappear as if by magic, believing they had only been gone a few hours? How could Aimee be here now, surrounded by ethereal dancers in a brilliant ballroom, if the stories–or at least a part of them–weren't true?

Aimee stepped out of the dance, and this time, he let her. He bowed with a sweeping arm, as if giving her permission to explore the room and discover the truth of his words. Guest after guest spun past her, faces twisted into mocking grins and formal wear twinkling in the light of the chandeliers. Suddenly, the room itself seemed to spin, and Aimee swayed with a wave of dizziness. Her heart pounded as her temples throbbed, her breathing coming in short gasps. That trapped feeling squeezed her once again, and she stumbled, pushing through the press of dancers for the fresher air beyond the main floor.

Bursting free of the waltzing couples, a glint of bright light caught her eye. A window frame beckoned, and she hurried for the far wall, intending to yell for help or climb to safety. But her hopes shriveled as she realized it was just a mirror reflecting the light of the room.

A woman stared back at her with hollowed cheeks and wild curls streaked with grey. Stepping closer, she squinted to examine the woman more carefully. The stranger, haggard and aging, was her own reflection. Cold fear filled her belly, sending a tremble down her limbs. Aimee entered the old theater ballroom as a 26-year-old woman. Now, in what felt like minutes, she looked the same age as her mother.

"No, no, what is happening?" Aimee wailed, pressing at the loosening skin on her cheeks and forehead as she stared at her reflection. "What have you done to me?"

"It is the price of joining the dance," the man said, appearing over her shoulder. "An hour a twirl, a month a waltz. These are the terms of entering our hall. The trickling seconds of your mortal life sustain the magic you so thanklessly enjoy."

"But I didn't know that when I walked through the door!" Aimee whirled on him. "There weren't any signs or notices. I didn't agree to any terms. I was just suddenly here."

His shoulders twitched in a minute shrug as a smile curled at his lips. "A notice is posted in magical runes on the doorjamb, if you bother to look. It's all above board."

"Magical runes? I can't read magical runes, much less see them, and I'll bet none of your other accidental guests could, either. That's not fair!"

"That's the rules."

Reining in her anger with a harsh breath, Aimee asked, "Then what are the rules for leaving?"

"Ah, finally, that is the correct question. Find my name, give it to me and you may leave."

"Give you your name?" Aimee repeated, frowning. She groaned. Riddles were a popular theme in fairy lore. Wordplay and double meanings masqueraded as guidelines. "So, if I can guess your name, I can leave?"

He nodded. "But tick-tock, my dear, or you'll run out of time."

Evie's agitation whenever the subject of names came up, even over something as simple as remembering her own, sprang to mind. Aimee imagined she'd faced this same dilemma during her stay in the ballroom. But Evie had eventually returned to reality, twice. That meant she had guessed correctly. And maybe, she had told Aimee the answer without her realizing it.

Digging the voice recorder from her pocket, Aimee played through her conversations with Evie. Finding himself ignored, the man shrugged again and returned to the dance floor, sweeping a new partner into his arms and melding back into the waltz.

Aimee stood on the edge, not looking at the guests, closing her eyes to the melodic orchestra, focusing only on the sound of Evie's voice. Finally, after too many precious minutes, the conversation turned towards Evie's escape.

"The party was wonderful. Magical. I never wanted to leave. But, I missed my family, my daughter's happy face. I wanted to go home. But *he* wouldn't let me. Kept me dancing. Twirling. Minute by minute. It took me hours and a turn with every one of his court before I finally sussed out what he wanted and gave it to him. He stole my life, that villain. *Wylde Hobbe.*"

Yes! She had him! She was free!

"Wylde Hobbe!" she called out, voice echoing along the walls, amplified enough to make the crystals hanging from the chandeliers tinkle. "I give you your name, now let me go home."

The music abruptly ended with the echo of his name, every dancer halting mid-step. Wylde Hobbe emerged from the dance floor, the faintest of lines creasing his brow the only sign of his anger she had won.

"Well done, dear. I accept my name with grace," he said with a bow. Straightening, he continued, "Would you do me the honor of extending me a kiss before you leave, to remember a wonderful dance partner?"

A kiss for an eternity. He had said that on their first waltz. He wasn't making a request, he was trying to trick her into surrendering the rest of her time.

"I'll just leave, thank you very much."

He smiled, rolling his eyes with a sigh. "Ah, well, it was worth a try. And do tell Evie I miss our time together. She was an exquisite dancer."

Wylde Hobbe pointed towards the left, and the wallpaper melted back to reveal the door. Aimee hesitated a moment, looking over her shoulder at the trio on the bench, sucked dry of their years and left to rot abandoned and forgotten. Her palms itched with the desire to scoop them up and drag them back with her, but a quick glance at the horde on the dance floor blocked that idea. The rules were clear, and Aimee was bound by them as long as she was on this side of the door.

With one last glance at the opulent room and the sparkling Host, Aimee ran for the door.

Getting her life back after twenty years in the ballroom had been no easy feat. When Aimee appeared back in the storage room of the theater, she barely recognized her old town. The theater itself had closed down years before, doors and windows boarded up. Her cellphone didn't have service, and her car was long gone. An entire generation had passed while she waltzed with the Fae.

At first, Aimee didn't even remember who she was, but with the help of her recordings, it came flooding back after a few minutes. That was the power of the portal between worlds: it jumbled up your memory until something brought it back.

Aimee hadn't left a spouse or children behind like Evie had, but there were still people who noticed her absence, people who resented her for leaving without a word. She knew better than to tell them the truth and end up in a care unit for the rest of her life. Instead, she spun a yarn about a secluded commune and two decades off the grid. It was easier for authorities to believe than a magical door transporting her to Fairyland. They took her statement, closed her missing-persons case, and sent her on her way.

Rebuilding what she had lost hadn't been as easy. Nothing was as she left it, not even her own body. The vitality and adventure of her youth had been siphoned away in another world, leaving her drained and bitter. There were days her regret at ever having met Evie—now long passed away—burned her soul, but most days she just felt empty.

On lonely nights while she lay in bed after a long day at the office, Aimee longed to return to that dazzling party, to forget her wasted years and revel in the enchantment for just a few more minutes. But then she remembered the desiccated, withering frames draped on the bench and reconsidered. The dance may have been magical, but her time was better spent right where she was. A life only half lived was still far more valuable than a waltz in time.

The End

Dead Spots

Whitney R. Holp

At the hotel Schlaffhaus, there were places known as "dead spots," places where radio signals could not be sent or received. Nobody knew about them except the hotel-staff, and only those who used the walkie-talkies. Perhaps a hotel-guest, wandering along with a portable transmitter, might have passed through one; but if they did, it was never reported. The hotel-management certainly had greater concerns than trying to locate these anomalies. And so, they remained, pockets of isolation within the building.

Nigel, the evening bellman there, knew about the dead spots. Indeed, he was warned about them during his first day on the job. He was hired as a summer student after the previous bellman inexplicably went missing. Karen, the woman who ran the front desk, took Nigel on a quick tour of the building and explained his duties. Whereupon she mentioned the dead spots.

"No one knows where they are," she said. "And no one really cares either. All it means is if you're in one, you can't hear anybody, and nobody can hear you. It probably has something to do with the wiring, stuff inside the walls. But anyway, unless you're in the lobby, you shouldn't be standing around. You should try to keep a move on."

Nigel nodded and said he understood. It was a pretty simple gig: all he had to do was patrol around and ensure nothing was amiss, carry luggage for guests when they arrived, deliver room service, and help with whatever else when asked. He was to check in at the front desk every hour, but otherwise he was left to his own initiative.

The dead spots, though a vivid notion, were nonetheless quickly forgotten.

After a few weeks, he thought he knew this place like the back of his hand. Yet he always marveled to discover a new doorway or secret stairwell – another shortcut to somewhere else, another piece of the puzzle. Once, he even happened upon an entire wing of the building abandoned for decades. Under a dust-caked sheet draped over a mass of shapes in the corner, he found a bunch of broken medical gear.

Subsequent to this discovery, Karen told him that this building used to be a hospital, before it was closed; later it was purchased by the hotel company and reopened. Nigel thought it notable that this place retained an aspect of transience among its occupants. Hospitals are places where people go to be born or to die (or be healed); now they only came here to stay a while, then go somewhere else.

The place had an oppressive air about it, common to both hotels and hospitals, that sickly electric light and residual chemical smell. Some nights, it was rather spooky wandering the seemingly endless corridors, passages of sterility. And in the early mornings, as he went about unlocking things for another day, opening the pool and banquet halls. The veil of reality seemed thinner on those occasions, the world less definite, as if it could somehow be smeared.

It came to pass that he spent more and more time at the hotel; he even started sleeping in the empty guest rooms instead of going home; he slept in his clothes. Sometimes, he dreamed about being there and wandering its halls just as he did when he was awake. (He might have even been sleepwalking in some cases, but he was the sort of person who would pass unnoticed most of the time anyway.)

One day, as he walked down a corridor toward the glowing neon-red exit sign, intending to take the stairs to the alley and smoke a cigarette, the gadget attached to his belt suddenly gave a static squelch and said, “Bellman, do you copy?”

He stopped and removed the walkie-talkie from its holster, pressed the button on its side, and said, “Bellman here.”

The gadget burped and said, “Bellman, we need to confirm a vacancy in Room 418.”

He pressed the button again and said, “Copy that. Over.”

The bellhop continued to the stairs, and went up instead of down. He almost never took the elevator. It was too much like teleporting: step inside, rattle and hum, then emerge on his destination. But, in fact, it was a steel death-cage of doom contained within a narrow drop. No, thank you. Taking the stairs was good exercise, too.

At the door of the fourth-floor landing, the walkie-talkie belched another burst of noise as he stepped through into the corridor, but Nigel barely noticed.

Meanwhile, in the lobby, Karen was paging him again. The reservation had been cancelled, so they didn’t need that room checked anymore. But there was no response from his end.

It was just as well, she supposed, that he didn’t know. This would give him something to do, and it would be good to verify the status of Room 418. She was worried about him though: the lad looked rather pale today. She tried paging him once more, then returned to filing reports on the computer.

Not much else was happening on this particular afternoon. Another boring summer day, just one of many. Though every suite had been booked, the hotel was rather quiet right now. The guests were mostly tourists and thus gone during the daylight hours.

Drifting from the restaurant down the hall, Karen could hear the murmured voices of not more than a dozen people. A few more puttered around in here, waiting for others to join them, but that was all.

Just then, a man walked into the lobby with a flamethrower.

Room 418 was clean. Nigel had keys to open every door in the hotel. He did a quick look around, seeing fresh linen, the beds made, all surfaces polished dust-free. It was a ready berth awaiting occupancy. He paged the front desk to inform them it was so, then started walking in search of another exit sign.

As he did, he glanced at his wrist-watch, wondering what time it was. On its face, he saw the seconds ticking past. Enough of those made a minute, and enough minutes made an hour, twenty-four of which were contained within a day, and days within weeks, weeks within months, months within years, and——

In the lobby, people were screaming. The madman locked the entrance and there was no way out. He streaked across the room, cackling laughter as he torched everything in sight. The furniture was in flames; the wallpaper dripped and curled off the walls. Waxen figures wailed as they melted, staggering, coughing, and crawling helplessly across the blood-smeared floor. Fire guttered in pockets of blistering flesh and smoldering fabric.

Time does not exist, thought Nigel. The whole notion was invented so that a third of a person's life was devoted to toil, and the forces that be could extract a financial gain from their efforts. We trade in our hours for a handful of dimes and money is the shit of time and time is an illusion. The present moment is all there really is.

At that moment, however, Nigel was more concerned with finding another of those glowing red exit signs. It had been quite a while since he left Room 418, and had been walking for so long now that he was rather hurting for another dose of nicotine. He cursed whoever had made smoking indoors illegal.

He slowed his pace to a stroll, wondering, with a vague sense of déjà-vu, if he hadn't come down this way already. It was impossible to be certain.

The corridors all looked the same, no matter which way he turned. Splitting off endlessly, one led to another, and from these were only more. He was lost in a maze of tapestried carpet subtly lit from above; the waist-high wood-paneling was topped with embroidered-looking wallpaper from there to the ceiling; and the rectangular doors, spaced evenly down the way, seemed to lead on into infinity.

Where is that damn exit, he wondered. *Really now*. And he continued his search.

Behind the front desk, Karen and the new guy, Wade, were crouched there listening. They could hear people on the other side, but it sounded like the lunatic had departed from their midst, for the moment at least. In his wake was only the shuffling of crippled heaps amid the wreckage and mewling caterwauls of those maimed by fire, those who knew pain but not death.

She heard more screams coming from the corridor that led to the restaurant. Wade crawled to the radio transmitter. Karen watched, knowing that before this, management had considered firing him, but also knowing that none of it mattered right now, not with the smoke drifting over the counter-top, and the rancid redolence of its stench.

He reached up and brought the device down to his face and spoke into it desperately:

"If anyone can hear this, GET OUT NOW! There's a maniac on the loose! He's killing everyone! Save yourselves——"

As Nigel approached a bend in the corridor, he heard a voice from around the corner say: "No! Not again! Don't come around here! Go away!"

But it was too late – he had rounded the corner. There, Nigel was faced with two human beings who looked like exact replicas of himself. They might have been clones or doppelgangers. Right down to the last detail: from the same mute dullard face and caesar-style haircut, to the company name-tag, cheap tie, and wristwatch.

He might have been looking in a mirror, were there not two of them. And also, the corridor behind them disappeared into a dimness of more shadows than dead light bulbs could account for.

One of the doppelgangers lit a cigarette.

"I don't fucking believe this," he said. "Why didn't you listen to me?"

Nigel was so flabbergasted he could hardly talk.

"What... who... huh?" he stammered.

"I told you not to come around here," said the doppelganger. "Now you can't leave. You're trapped here forever."

"Or until the monster eats you," said the second one and lit a cigarette.

"Don't say I didn't warn you," said the first one.

Nigel stared at them incredulously. Then he said, "This is fucked," and turned to leave.

As he did, however, he sensed something move quickly up behind him, grabbing his lower leg and yanking back so hard that he fell. He landed on his hands and knees and looked back in time to see as a large tentacle uncoiled from around his ankle and slithered back into the shadows.

Nigel waited until it was gone before he got back to his feet.

"This is fucked," he repeated and stared at the doppelgangers, and they stared back at him.

"Let's just hope you pay more attention next time," the second one said.

Nigel looked around, then he sighed, and lit a cigarette of his own. There was no sense not to.

The rest of the world was out there and happening; he was here right now.

The End

The Arbour

Lasalina Tess

Leaves rustle in the cool autumn breeze, creating a myriad of random melodies that even crickets would struggle to follow. A gust of wind seeps through the holes of my knitted blue sweater, and I hug myself to keep warm while I walk between birch trees. The last time I was here, I was twelve years old. Auntie Carol would chase me through the forest with a bucket that held water balloons; filled and ice-cold. She had terrible aim, which made it even more fun. While I ran, I heard her shouting, "Meagan, you little shit, you're too fast!"

That was thirteen years ago; two months before she disappeared.

Although I don't recall each tree with intimate detail, they're familiar and bring me comfort, like old friends or a fully stocked bookshelf that brings me joy. The pathway that was once cleared of foliage has now grown over and difficult to follow. Yet, I continue forward, listening to the leaves and birds, enjoying nature's beauty.

Late evening sunbeams shine between the treetops and it's mesmerizing. A green glimmer catches my gaze to the right, a few feet from the path, and I head towards it. Twigs snap beneath my runners as I squeeze through the narrow opening between two birch trees. Poison ivy redirects me, but I find my way closer to the source of the green light. It's higher than expected, dangling from a black metal arbour.

I stop in front of the old archway that is coated with spiderwebs and laced with vines. The green glimmer reflects off a gemstone, or crystal-like object. It's embedded into the centre, at the very top of the arbour. What is it, emerald maybe? It's the size of the palm of my hand, so if it's real, then it's probably worth a fortune. If I were desperate enough, I'd pry it out, but it's perfect exactly where it is. Maybe I can bring a couple of friends back here and take the whole arbour home. It would look beautiful in my garden. Why didn't Auntie Carol ever show me this? Unless she didn't know it existed, or if it was placed here after her disappearance.

The dark green vines weave through the sides of the arbour with thorns and wilted leaves. My gaze reaches the ground, where there appears to be a flower bud. I kneel for a closer look. It's a rose, but this late in the season? What's stranger still is that the petals peering through the bud are blue. A rich cerulean. I am not a pro with flowers, but I know that natural blue roses do not exist. The only way to make one this colour is by dyeing them. Someone went through a lot of effort with this arbour.

As I reach for the rosebud, my fingers tingle, so I pull away and move my shoulder around; maybe I pinched a nerve at some point. Again, I reach for the flower and the tingling returns and as my fingertip touches the bud, heat floods into my hand. The wave spreads up my arm, through my shoulder, along my back and extends to every inch of my body. My first instinct is to pull away, but I can't move. Even breathing becomes difficult. A scream swells in my throat, but nothing escapes my lips. It's like becoming a statue. Made of fire.

The heat intensifies. My vision blurs. The world spins around me and becomes dark. Suddenly, I'm moving, but I can't see where I'm going. What is happening? Did I faint? Was the rose poisonous?

Movement ceases.

The heat fades to a lingering warmth, like a fleece blanket wrapped around me, and I'm no longer in constant motion. Senses return to normal. No longer am I a statue stuck in place. Instead, I'm laying on the ground, while blades of grass tickle my fingers and poke through my sweater. At last, I open my eyes. When did I close them? Above me, branches sway beneath the clear blue sky, with leaves a vibrant green, unlike the nearly bare branches from a moment ago. The dizziness passes, and I sit upright, holding my head. To my left is the same arbour, only it is clear of any webs, and blue roses are in full bloom along the vines. Where am I?

There are no birch trees or multi-coloured, crunchy fall leaves. There's no pathway or semblance of familiarity. How is this possible? How can I go from being in the heart of fall to returning to mid-summer? I slip off my sweater and lay it in the grass. It's too hot to keep it on.

A rustling distracts me straight ahead. Someone is running through the forest; or something. I stand and find my balance, preparing for whoever, or whatever, is coming closer. Bushes part and a figure stumbles into the small clearing. His nose looks crooked and grey. Breathing heavily, he meets my gaze. His black eyes narrow and he grips the handle of his axe tighter. My heartrate thunders in my ears, drowning out all other sounds. The inhuman creature raises the axe and calls out a terrible cry as he races in my direction.

Stumbling, I turn and run into the unfamiliar forest. The creature is shorter than me, if I'm lucky my long legs will carry me faster than he can follow. Without the crisp sounds of dried leaves on the ground, it's impossible to hear his footsteps over my own. The grass is damp and the ground soft. Tall, dark brown tree trunks whirl past me. I jump over small bushes and turn to the left, hoping he's far enough behind that he doesn't notice that I've changed direction. Who or what is he? He is extremely old or not from this planet. Are aliens real?

An enormous pile of boulders catches my gaze. I rush to the other side of them and drop to my hands and knees. A warm hand clasps my mouth, and a powerful arm pulls me against a firm body.

"Stay quiet," the male voice whispers.

I squirm and fight to break free, but it's of no use. The man holding me is much stronger. From his hand, I inhale an earthy scent: A blend of soil, herbs and florals. A farmer? The grey-skinned figure passes the boulders and continues forward a few paces before stopping.

The man holding me whispers in my ear, "stay still."

I nod. What other choice do I have?

The man releases me and slides away, moving slowly forward like a shadow growing beneath the sunset. A green hooded cloak conceals his identity, but it's clear that he is taller than I am. His arm reaches back over his right shoulder, and without a moment's hesitation he throws a knife. It plunges into the grey one's skull with a sick crunch, sending a splatter of dark liquid behind it.

The creature's body drops hard to the ground.

My breath quickens. This can't be real. Did I hit my head on the arbour? On a rock? Maybe I'm still laying near the birch trees in a bed of leaves, and the arbour never existed. Either way, dream or not, it feels real, and I must escape. Yet, if I run, this man would likely kill me in the same manner, and staying here doesn't seem safe either. What else can I do?

The hooded man faces me and reaches out a hand. I stare at the long slender fingers; the same fingers that are capable of murder without regret. "I won't hurt you," he says. "But there are more of them nearby. We must leave. Now."

My gaze drifts to meet his vibrant green eyes, and his perfect face. Not a mole or pimple exists on his tanned skin. Nor a scar or any other blemish.

"You can trust me," he continues. "Please, hurry."

Whether it's the urgency in his voice, or an instinct deep down that has awakened inside me, I'm not sure, but I take his hand. He pulls me to my feet and leads me through the trees. We run as fast as possible sticking to the densest areas for cover. The whole while the sensation of being watched creeps down my back. Branches scratch my bare arms, and every few steps I duck to avoid low-hanging branches. Thankfully, wearing jeans protects my legs, although they are plastered to me from sweat.

At last, we stop at a tree to catch our breath. "Who are you?" I say, between gasps for air.

The man watches the direction we came from for any sign of movement. "Larren," he replies.

"I'm Meagan."

Larren nods. "I think they've headed West."

How many of them are there? Feeling drained, I kneel in the grass next to him. "What was that guy?" I say. "He wasn't... he didn't look... human."

Without responding, he pushes his hood off. Larren's long brown hair is tied at the nape of his neck, and his ears rise to a point. His large green eyes seem to glow like there's hidden lightbulbs beneath them, reminding me of that stone that glimmered at the top of the arbour.

Numbness spreads through me, and I pull away, eager to put space between us. "Neither do you..." I am drawn to the intense green of his eyes. They call to me, as if I've been waiting to see them all my life. A face I've never seen before, not even in my dreams. How could I long to meet this individual, long to be near him, without being aware of his existence? Every inch of his body appeals to me, makes me wish to never leave his side. If this is a dream, may I never wake.

Larren smiles, like he knows how I'm feeling. "No, I'm not human, and neither was he, but you are." His gaze drifts over me. "How did you get here?"

The birch forest surfaces in my thoughts. "I'm not entirely sure, to be honest." My voice is weak, the shock apparent in my tone.

I clear my throat, pouring all focus into his question. "I found this beautiful arbour and when I touched the blue rose, everything spun. Then I woke up here."

Larren's eyes widen. "The portal; you've found it."

"Portal?" The word does much to explain my experience. Could it be real? Could all of this be real, including Larren?

His expression changes and he reaches out to me. "Come on."

Not again. "Where are we going now?" I've finally caught my breath and from all the commotion I just want to find a quiet place to hide.

"There's someone else, a friend, who needs to find that portal before it disappears again." Larren gestures for me to take his hand. "And I'm sure you'll want to get back."

Another human maybe? With a sigh, I stand and slide my hand into his, and then we're off once more, running through the dense forest. It feels like it has taken forever when we finally stop at the side of a large hill that is surrounded by trees. Larren pushes branches aside to reveal an opening in the hill, resembling a cave. It's dark inside. I can't see a thing, but at least it isn't deep, and I have Larren to guide me. Although we've just met, I think I can trust him. He did save my life after all.

"Are you there?" Larren whispers.

"Yes," a woman answers. "Are they gone?"

Larren releases my hand, leaving me to stand in the darkness. "They are," he says. "For now, at least."

There's a scraping sound, and a flicker of light, then a small blue flame erupts on the ground. It takes a moment for my eyes to adjust, but when they do, the woman's face startles me. "Auntie Carol?"

The woman examines me and moves around the fire to touch my face. "Meagan? Is that really you?" She pulls me into her arms. "How did you get here?"

Tears stream down my cheeks and reach my lips creating a salty taste in my mouth. "I must be dreaming."

Auntie Carol releases me and grasps my shoulders, her face damp from crying. "Trust me, this is not a dream, girl. I've been trying to find a way home for so long."

Larren clears his throat, interrupting our moment. "She came through the portal."

"But you said it moves, are you sure it's still there?" Auntie Carol says, glancing between the two of us.

"There's only one way to find out," Larren says. "We must be fast. I'll make sure it's safe first." He leaves the hill-cave.

"You've grown." Aunt Carol runs a hand along my arm. "How long have I been here? There aren't exactly calendars nearby."

Memories flash through my mind of volunteers searching the woods. Posters of her face plastered all over town. Mom's therapy appointments. I force a smile. "Thirteen years."

She gasps. "No wonder. I counted the days, but I stopped once I accepted the fact that I may never get home." Auntie shakes her head, and her gaze drifts away.

Maybe she found the same portal that I did. "The arbour. Did you come through the arbour?"

Auntie Carol nods. "Yes, and I've looked for it repeatedly... but it was just... gone. Larren taught me how to survive here. I've been moving from hiding place to hiding place, hoping that one day the portal would return. I'd almost given up." She smiles and pats my arm. "But you're here now, which means it's back."

It's difficult to see much of her in this cave, but I can tell she's lost a lot of weight, and the odd silver strand in her hair reflects the blue glow from the flame. "It must have been terrifying for you," I say. "Trapped here for so long."

Before Auntie can reply, Larren pokes his head in the entrance. "Ready?"

Together, we stand, and Auntie stomps out the small flame, then we leave the cave. The lighting in the forest has dimmed, and the sunset on the horizon creates a red-purple glow all around us. With Aunt Carol's firm grasp on my own, a sense of security fills me. So many lost years. What will we tell people once we're back? They'll think we're crazy.

The arbour is exactly where I left it, only the blue roses are closing.

"Hurry," Larren says. "Go through."

Aunt Carol pulls Larren into her arms. "Thank you, my friend. For everything. Maybe one day we'll meet again."

She releases their embrace, and Larren moves closer to me. "This isn't a safe place for humans, but if you ever return, I'll be here."

My stomach flutters. "Thank you for looking after my aunt."

Larren bows. "It was my pleasure."

My gaze lingers with his until Aunt Carol pulls me towards the arbour and before I know it, the world spins, then darkens, as the portal carries us from one world to another. Warmth fills my body, but it quickly fades when we stop moving. We lay side by side on the dry ground, surrounded by birch trees. Between the branches above, stars speckle the black sky.

A cool breeze reminds me I forgot to grab my sweater. Maybe Larren will look after it for me. A tension tightens around us, like the air is getting thinner. Aunt Carol pulls me to my feet and drags me away from the arbour. From behind a tree, we watch as the portal is sucked inward, like it's folding inside of itself. Leaves fly toward it, vanishing as they encounter the metal bars.

"Hold onto me," Auntie Carol says.

The wind strengthens and sucks everything it can into the portal's grasp. A flash of light, then calm. We approach the location where the arbour once stood and find nothing but dirt. Even the grass was uprooted. At least the trees still stand.

We meet each other's gaze and smile. "You're really here," I say.

She nods, tears in constant flow. "It's been far too long, my girl." Auntie Carol pulls me into her arms. The woman may be thinner, but her strength has tripled.

"What will we tell everyone?" I say, pulling myself from her grasp. "No one would believe the truth." The fresh scrapes on my arms sting in the cool air.

With a shrug, she says, "I went walk-about."

We laugh, and hug once more.

"Can we go home now?" she says. "I haven't seen my cats in so many years. Are they okay?"

With a sigh, I link my arm with hers. "We have a lot to talk about." Arm in arm, we return to the path and begin the adventure of catching up on the past thirteen years.

The End

The Wish in a Box: Part One

Rebecca Hunnie

Carla sits on her bed, legs dangling over the edge. The black walls are lined with images of her and her friends. The latest party was in the works, and she was waiting for the details.

"Carla Hope Erickson, get down here!" her mother yells, interrupting her intense focus. "I will be right there, mom!" she shouts back.

Hopping off her bed, something tickles Carla's ankle. She brushes it off and then rushes down the stairs.

"What's going on?" she asks her mom.

"You ditched school today?" her mom says with an angry tone.

"Chill, I had gym class, and we were doing fitness testing." Carla shrugs off her mom's anger.

"You know better, you will be making up that testing at school when you go back," her mom scolds.

"Whatever," Carla says stomping away.

"Get back here!" her mother yells.

"What!?" Carla barks.

"You are grounded for three days. No going out, no friends over. You go straight to school and straight home. You got it?" Her mother holds her ground; arms folded across her chest.

"What, for skipping school, are you kidding me?" Carla challenges.

"No. You will be very lucky if I don't take your phone." Her mother snarls while taking a sip of her tea.

"Whatever!" She stalks toward her room. "I wish I lived with dad," she says over her shoulder.

"What was that?" her mother shouts.

Once in her room, Carla digs her phone out of her pocket. The message reads: *Party Friday night at Sienna's, her parents are out of town!*

Creating a quick reply she sits on her bed. *Perfect, just got grounded, meet me down the street so my mom doesn't see.* Crossing the room she sits at her desk, then selects her music playlist to begin her homework.

The evening flies by as Carla finishes up her algebra and tucks her books away. Getting ready for bed, something tickles her ankle again. She slips onto the floor and lifts her blanket. "Hmmm, nothing there." She grabs the flashlight from the top drawer of her nightstand to inspect a little further. Turning it on, she shines it under the bed and sees a purple box. "Where did this come from?" She asks herself, taking out the sparkly shoebox. She sits back on her bed and places the box beside her. What is mom's problem? I wish I never lived here; she is so mean. Returning her focus to the box, she runs her fingers around the edge of the lid. Opening it a crack, there's something fuzzy inside. The box lights up, her room goes dark, and she blacks out.

Carla wakes up disoriented.

The lighting in her room has returned to normal, only she is no longer at her mother's. Instead, she's in her room at her dad's place. How did I get here? The mysterious box sits on the nightstand beside her bed. None of this makes sense.

"Carla, can you come here please?" her dad calls out from down the hall.

"Umm, sure thing dad. I'll be right there!" Carla says shaking her head. She gets off her bed and heads to the kitchen. In the doorway she inspects her dad. His hair is grayer and is shorter. She notices more images of her and her friends and her dad with a blonde woman.

"Dad, what's going on?"

"What do you mean dear?" he says with a chuckle.

"How did I get here?"

"Honey, what are you muttering about?" He gently taps her temple. "Did you hit your head?"

"I was just in my room, at home." Carla explains.

"You are home!" He says, confusion painted across his face.

As she sits down at the table, Carla notices her school picture on the counter, and a vase of purple and pink flowers.

"I was just in my room," she repeats. "The box, where did the box go?"

"Carla, what is going on, should I call a doctor? You aren't making any sense."

"Dad, I was just in my room at home. I mean at mom's." Carla gazes around the room, her gaze pausing at an image of her and her mom from ten years ago. "How did I get here?"

"You haven't seen your mom in over a year," he says, taking a seat at the table.

"What are you talking about? She just grounded me for ditching gym class." A chuckle escapes her.

"Gym... you haven't been at school in five years. We took a vacation, remember?"

Carla shakes her head. "I swear I was just in my room, at home, with mom. I was grounded." Laughter consumes her.

"Carls, are you okay?"

"Forget it, what did you need me for?" she says, shaking her head.

"Ana was wondering if you would like to go get your nails done?" he explains. "She just called."

"Umm. Ana?" Carla asks scratching her head.

"Your stepmom?" His eyebrows raise in confusion. "Blonde, just came back from holidays with us, we have been married a little over two years. Anything ring a bell?"

Carla paces the kitchen. She looks at the photos on the fridge, opens the door and grabs a soda. “May I?”

“Since when, do you ask for a soda?” he says.

“Dad?” Carla raises her eyebrow.

“Are you sure you’re, okay?” Worry is apparent in his expression as he sits in a chair.

Carla shakes her head and returns to her room to find it exactly how she left it: Clean, organized and sans a purple box. The display on her cell phone shows April 17th, 2030. “What in the world?” she says to the empty room. Her phone dings in her hand. The message reads: *You missed a killer party last night, Cara totally puked. Message me when you get back from holidays. Love you girl! ~Alexis*

She replies to her friend. *I thought the party was Friday?*

*No, yesterday, are you back now or what? ~A *

Between messages with Alexis, Carla looks around her room for anything to explain how she got to her dads and how she lost a whole ten years. Without any luck, she heads back to the kitchen. “Dad, what happen with mom?”

“What do you mean?” he answers.

“Why did I end up here, with you? What happened with mom?” She cracks open her soda.

“Your mother and I believed this would be the best thing for you. She was dealing with some stressors and ultimately, we left the decision up to you, and you chose to stay here. You and your friends see a lot of each other still and Alexis is here.” Her dad tries to help her understand.

“Speaking of Alexis, she messaged me, do you mind if I go see her?” she asks warily.

"Sure, honey. Did you give some thought into what I asked you earlier?" he says, as Carla gets up to leave.

"Alright, dad, I would love to go get my nails done with Ana!" she says excitedly.

"Great, I will let her know." Her dad turns away.

As Carla heads back to her room, she messages Alexis using dictation. *Home from holidays and heading over, are you home?*

Yup. The message reads back.

Confusion overwhelms Carla, but taking a deep breath, she grabs her keys, phone, and handbag, then leaves her room.

Alexis greets her when she arrives with a warm, friendly hug, and then they head inside. "How were your holidays, where did you go, did you bring me anything?" Alexis fires off.

"Whoa, slow down! I don't remember, it is so weird. I remember being in my room, I mean at my mom's, she had just grounded me." Carla shakes her head. "I know this sounds crazy."

"Okay, hold on. The last time you saw your mom was over a year ago," Alexis explains. "She was not well; she was always so angry. You told me you were fighting, and she told you to get out."

"What? Why didn't my dad tell me that?" she says. "When did you add purple to your hair, Lex?"

"Maybe he is protecting you from her, or her from you?" Alexis adds, taking Carla's hand and leading her through the house.

As the girls enter Alexis' bedroom, Carla tries to remember seeing her mom last. She recalls being grounded for ditching class and talking to her friend about a party. In the room, music plays, pulling her attention from her thoughts. "Last Night by Morgan Wallen, right?" she says.

"Yes, it is our favourite song." Alexis laughs. "What did you mean I look different?"

"Of course, I knew that." Carla chuckles. "You had darker hair, and it was longer. Lex, can you tell me, are things good with my dad and Ana?"

"Ana has been great for you and your dad," Alexis tells her.

"It has been a year since I talked to my mom. What happened?"

"You and your mom just didn't see eye to eye. You were a rebellious teen, and she wanted to control you. She soon realized that it wasn't going to happen, so she told you to get out," Alexis explains. "Are you okay?"

"Lex, I remember my mom being a little protective; but controlling, that doesn't seem right. I know her divorce from my dad was rough, but I can't see her kicking me out." Carla shakes her head.

"Sweetie, you were a teen, you wanted to do whatever you wished, but she wanted you safe. Ten years ago, when you were in high school, we both found the wrong crowds. Now look at us, fully employed, strong friendship and you and Damien have been together for three years. Do you remember any of this?"

"Damien?"

"Yes, you guys began dating three years ago when you met in college. Don't tell me you don't remember Damien?" Concern is clear across Alexis's face.

"Whoa, slow down. Boyfriend, college, employed, and stability... how; I mean when?" Carla asks, rattled.

"Take a seat my friend, let me get you a glass of water, you look pale," Alexis says, motioning for Carla to sit down.

As Alexis leaves for the nearby bathroom, Carla sits at the desk nearby. Browsing the pictures on the desk she comes across one of her and a guy. "Who is that?" she asks when Alexis returns.

"Here," Alexis says, handing her the water before picking up the picture. "This is you and Trevor, do you remember Trevor?"

"From high school?" Carla says, focusing on the face in the photo.

"Yes, we all used to hang out together. He drifted away from us a few years ago after he and I dated. It ended mutually, we both needed space."

"Wait, you and Trev? Wow, did I miss a lot. So, what's the deal with Damien and I?" she asks her friend curiously. "What does he look like, how long have we been together?"

"You and Damien met in college, we all kind of started hanging out together and he was always very sweet to you."

Carla's cheeks flush with warmth.

Alexis gasps playfully. "Are you blushing?"

"No." Carla covers her face, letting out a girly shriek of happiness.

"Carla, you know I have your best interests at heart, right?" Alexis says.

"Of course, I do! Why do you ask?"

"Just want to make sure, you know."

Both girls chuckle.

"Always so humble!" Carla bursts out laughing like a hyena. Once she's able to breathe and calm herself, she asks, "So, when is the next party?"

"Well, Damien and I were talking about that. We weren't sure when you were coming back, but we were thinking Saturday at Xander's."

"Xander?" Carla says.

"Damien's best friend." Alexis laughs. "I keep forgetting, did you bump your head over the holidays or something?"

"Or something!" Carla laughs with her friend. "I should go, my dad said something about Ana and getting our nails done together."

"Nails, you're just back from vacay, and you didn't get them done there?"

Looking down at her hands, Carla inspects her sparkly blue nails and matching toes. "Weird, you are right." She laughs. "I wonder what the stepmom is up to?"

They both laugh together.

As Carla gets in her car, she can't help but think about how she ended up ten years in the future. With a boyfriend, a career and living with her dad; it is the life she has always wanted. A life filled with peace, happiness and love. Things were complicated at mom's; she always wanted to pick a fight. Carla turns on the music and "My Wish" by the Rascal Flatts comes on. A song that her and her mom used to listen to when one of them would have "Big Feelings", as her mom called them. Arriving back at her dad's place she pulls in the driveway and sees a purple Jeep Wrangler.

"Who is that?" she asks herself, as she gets out of her car.

Inside, she finds her dad in the kitchen with a tall blonde wearing a short red dress. "Dad?" Carla shouts.

"Hi, sweetie. Ana was just wondering when you were going to be home." He kisses the woman's forehead.

"Oh, right, I just noticed my nails are done already. Can you excuse me?" she says, rushing off to her room. Carla searches frantically looking for a box. "Nope, not that one," she says, chucking box after box over her shoulder from her closet.

Not long after, her parents walk in and ask what she's doing.

"I must find that box," she tells them.

"What box, Carla, are you okay?" Ana asks, worry etched on her face.

"I am fine, I just need to find that box. I never meant for her to be out of my life for good." Carla rattles off.

"What, who? Who did you never mean to be out of your life for good?" her father asks with a note of concern in his voice.

"Hey, let's go out for dinner. You pick!" Ana says kindly.

"I need to find it," Carla repeats.

"Find what?" her dad says.

"Nothing, can I have some privacy please?" she gestures for them to leave.

"Carls, sweetie I am worried about you," her dad says. "First you don't remember anything, then you are looking for something so frantically that you can't come have a conversation with us, and now you're kicking us out of your room."

"Dad, I am fine, I just need to find something that I lost." As they walk towards her, she raises her hands to stop them.

"As long as you are sure that you are okay," he adds before leaving her room.

Kneeling beside her bed, Carla lifts the blanket back hoping to see something that doesn't belong. She is met with nothing.

A while later, Ana calls from the kitchen. "Carla, dinner is ready!"

"I will be right there!" she shouts back. Her phone dings: * Where are you? * I can't deal with you right now, she thinks.

"I know I said wished I lived here, but this is just not my life. I do not remember any of it." Carla gets off the floor.

Heading down the hall for dinner, she is met by a dog. "Hi big guy!" she says, patting his head.

"Scruffy, you named him when we got him," her dad explains.

"Right, hi Scruffy," Carla says, heading towards the kitchen as a familiar aroma fills the air.

"Garlic shrimp and mushroom alfredo for dinner. Is that okay?" Ana asks, gazing around the room.

"That is my favorite," Carla says, taking a seat on a nearby barstool.

"Here," Ana says, offering her breadsticks.

"Thank you," Carla says, taking one and dipping it into her pasta.

While they eat, the table is met with silence, until her dad asks, "Any plans tomorrow?"

"No, why?" Carla asks, curious.

"I thought we would take a small trip to see the canyon, maybe go swimming. We have something we wanted to talk to you about."

"I don't know dad, we just got back. I think I want to just relax and see my friends." Carla tries to dodge more family time, which has become her new mission.

"Carla, sweetie, are you sure you're, okay?" Ana says.

"I'm fine, I just don't want to talk about it." Carla finishes her dinner and leaves the table.

I was with my mom this morning. How did I get here? What is going on with my dad? As she makes it back to her room, she continues searching for anything that will take her back. Back to her room, her mom and her friends. She sits down beside her bed and lifts the sheet once more. It must be here.

Awhile later, Carla crawls into bed and watches TV, a welcomed distraction as she tries to fall asleep.

The next morning, she hears her phone going crazy. *What happen to you last night? Alexis told me you were back. ~D *

*Where are you? ~A *

Whoa I must have crashed hard. Carla gets out of bed rubbing her eyes, and heads to the bathroom. Man, what is going on? She washes her hands and face with a warm cloth. Back in her room, the phone rings. "Hello?" she answers, putting the call on speaker so she can get dressed.

"Where are you?" the male voice asks her.

"Hi babe, I'm at home, just waking up," Carla answers, hoping to sound convincing.

"Why didn't you answer me last night?" Damien says.

"Babe, I was having such a weird night. I crashed early. Do you want to come over?"

"I need to work, but I am off around two, do you want to meet for lunch? At the square food truck?" he says, sounding hopeful.

"I'll see you there," she says before hanging up. Carla grabs a white flowery dress from her closet and a pair of dark blue tights. Slipping it over her head, she hears a knock at her door.

"Carls, I just want to make sure you are, okay?" her dad says through the door.

"Fine dad, just getting dressed."

"Can you stay for breakfast? I made waffles and bacon!" he shouts with enthusiasm.

"I am late for meeting Lex, raincheck?" she says, opening the door and rushing past him down the hall.

"Sure, but be safe please," he calls after her.

Just as she reaches her car, her phone buzzes. *Where are you, we were supposed to have breakfast. ~A* she reads.

Carla answers with: *Running late, slept in sorry. On my way.*

At the restaurant, Alexis is already seated at a table along the wall. A light wave of her hand, and Carla walks towards her, and then takes a seat across from her. "Morning sleepyhead," Carla says. "I really don't know what happened, Lex, am I making sense?"

"Carla, slow down. You just got here. Grab a coffee and we can weed through this. What is going on?" Alexis says with a hint of worry.

"Nothing about this is what it should be. I opened a box, and I was brought here. Ten years into the future. I know this doesn't make sense but yesterday when I woke up, I was fifteen years old and grounded by my mom for skipping gym class."

"Wait, I remember that," Alexis says, nodding. "We had fitness testing, right?"

"Yes, you told me about a party at Sienna's," Carla replies. "What ever happened to her?"

Alexis points her finger, directing Carla's attention behind her.

The waitress approaches their table. "Welcome to Johnnies, my name is Sienna what can I start you off with?"

"Sienna, how are you?" Carla says.

"Cut the crap," Sienna snaps, pouring her a cup of coffee.

"What?" Carla says, confused.

"Why are you here?" Sienna continues.

"To... eat...." Carla says, cautiously, as Sienna walks away. Facing Alexis, she says, "Explain?"

"A couple years ago, Sienna dated Damien. We all used to be friends, but she grew resentful when Damien broke things off." Alexis turns the handle of her coffee cup and takes a sip.

"Of me? What did I do?" Carla asks.

"You know Sienna. She is all about the dramatics." Alexis giggles.

"Lex, does she blame me for their breakup?" Carla says, adding sugar to her coffee.

"Yes, but it wasn't your fault." Alexis pats Carla's hand to reassure her.

"You know what? It doesn't matter. I was trying to tell you that when I opened this box, I was brought here. Now, I can't find this box, it was in my room at my moms, and I could swear it was on the nightstand. But, after dinner I went to check, and it was gone." Carla fights back the tears swelling in her eyes.

"I mean, it sounds like you won the parental jackpot. You have two parents who were not so good together, you get into a fight with your mom and wake up happy and thriving at your dads." Alexis's humour is almost annoying.

"Lex, I never meant for my mom to be permanently out of my life. Yes, we have our differences, but that doesn't mean I wanted her out completely," Carla says sounding somber.

Alexis sighs. "I remember that call, I told you there was a party. When I came to pick you up, your mom had upset you again. Car, you were in tears. She said that you were disappointing her with your choices, and you stormed out. We went to that party together and you just wanted to sit there. I let you have your space because I knew you needed to process what she said. As hard as it was to see you that way, I watched you rise."

"Wow, I don't remember anything aside from being grounded and you telling me about the party. Did my mom and I fight lots?" Carla could guess what the answer would be.

"Not all the time, but when you did, it was volatile," Alexis explains.

Carla sits back in the chair, listening as her friend tries to help her understand. Grasping her cup of coffee, she shakes her head. The girls get up to leave and Carla puts money on the table. She sees Sienna on the way out. She mouths, "Please, call me. I would like to talk."

After saying goodbye to Alexis, Carla drives away, continuing to try and piece together how she got here. Once at home, she goes to her room and sits on her bed in tears. I never meant for this to happen.

There's a knock on her bedroom door.

"Come in!" She shouts.

"Carla, are you alright?" Ana asks as she enters.

"It wasn't supposed to be this way." Tears slide down Carla's face.

"What, sweetie?" Her stepmom seems baffled as she wraps an arm around Carla.

"I never meant to wipe her out of my life; I was just so mad." Carla wipes the tears from her eyes and cheeks.

"Carla, what are you saying?" Ana asks, sounding even more confused.

"My mom, I never meant for my mom to be out of my life for good," Carla says, getting up to grab a tissue.

"What's bringing this on, sweetie?" Ana's eyes widen with concern.

"You will think I'm crazy," Carla says, avoiding her gaze.

"Carla, please?" she pleads, like she's trying to help.

They sit next to each other on the bed.

"Yesterday, when my mom got home from work, she was so mad," Carla explains. "I ditched school, and I said something I shouldn't have said."

"Yesterday? You were on vacation with your father and I," Ana says.

"I know this sounds crazy, yesterday for me was ten years ago. I was in my room after talking to my mom. She had just grounded me." A tear slips down her cheek again.

"Carla, this doesn't make sense." Ana wipes Carla's cheek with her thumb.

"I know, I sound crazy. But there was this purple box, I was mad that my mom grounded me for ditching class, I said something..." she pauses looking up at the ceiling trying not to cry again, but it's no use. She drops her head into her hands and sobs.

Ana wraps her arm around her shoulder. "Carla, what is going on? What did you say?"

"I didn't mean it... she must know I didn't mean it. I would never mean it," Carla says. "I wish I could take them back."

"Sweetie, what did you say?" Ana says.

"I told her I wished I live with my dad." Carla looks up at Ana wiping her face. "And now here I am, and she probably hates me."

"Your mom, she could never hate you. Mothers are all wired to love their children, unconditionally." Ana grabs a tissue for Carla.

"I can remember her face; she was so broken." Carla takes the tissue from Ana. "Thank you."

"Carls, I haven't known you long, but I know how close you and your mom were. Your father told me some things, and please believe me, whatever happened didn't have anything to do with you."

"What things?" Carla says.

"It's not important, what is important is that you remember all the love you have for her. She will come back when she is ready, she just had a lot going on." Ana offers Carla a water bottle.

"How do you know?" she asks her stepmom.

"Because I am a mom, too, and I can't imagine being away from you forever. You are such a wonderful, smart, and caring young woman. You have grown so much in the short time I have known you and I couldn't be prouder of you." Ana grasps Carla's hands in hers.

"I just wish I could take those words back." A tickle brushes Carla's ankle. "Would you excuse me?" She stands and walks toward the closet.

"Sure, let me know if you need anything," Ana says, getting up to leave. She closes the door behind her.

Carla crosses the room to her bed and lifts her blanket. "Please, be under here. Please," she pleads, ducking under her bed.

Turning the flashlight on, she looks around under the bed. Something sparkly catches her eye. A thrill of excitement rushes through her. Using the broom from beside her closet, Carla slides it out from deep under her bed. "Oh, my goodness. Please take me back. I want to see my mom." She opens the box and finds pictures of her and her mom. With her eyes glued to an image of them together, disappointment washes over her. Nothing happens. She's still stuck in the future at her dad's. Sighing, Carla climbs into bed and continues examining the photos, wishing she could see her mom one more time.

Nightfall hits and her head drops onto the pillow.

Morning arrives, and as her eyes open, Carla is confused again. "Now where am I?" She says out loud rubbing her eyes.

"Carla, you are going to be late!" the familiar woman's voice shouts.

"Mom, is that you?" She calls back.

"Are you okay?" Her mom asks, rushing into the room.

"How did I get back here?"

"Back where, honey? You aren't making sense." Her mom sits down beside her.

"Mom!" She embraces her mother warmly.

As Carla tries to explain, her mom stares with a bizarre expression. Carla looks down and sees the purple box with a note taped to it that reads:

"Do not wish to be anything but what you are and try to be that perfectly." Saint Francis de Sales.

To be continued...

A Short Drive

T. M. Heinrichs

What if they're lying, and this really is a plan to kill us? Lisa stepped out of the port-a-potty onto the hot tarmac of Staging Area for Group 27.

The August sky had smears of clouds; the slight breeze only made the metallic smell of exhaust worse. She stared at the semi trucks, there were hundreds, no thousands, *if the stories are true,* pulling into the staging area. Most, not all, would have been built in 1987 or earlier because that was the last year the semi-trucks came computer free. Turning, the hot afternoon sun glinted on chrome, windshields, and paint that came in every colour. She watched as more trucks pulled onto the tarmac. Some were from the early 1990s, they had been modified to remove the computers and made completely analog, apparently it hadn't been hard – *if they are telling the truth.*

All the trailers were closed in or soon would be. Four trailers full of cattle passed by, the cows staring with their huge eyes. Their scent mixed with the smell of other trailers of livestock. Groups of men, most young, climbed up and began closing the rubberized covers. One trailer had horses that were snorting as they pulled passed, and the sound of sheep bleating grew loud as she walked down the line. Those organizing waited until the last minute before closing in the livestock trailers, so the animals didn't overheat. They had been told that every livestock trailer had a huge, pressurized tank of oxygen attached to the top, and there they were.

Ahead was a blue 1992 Freightliner, she only knew the year because Rita, the driver's wife, had told her. Though the Freightliner logo – *is it called a logo?* – gave it away. They didn't have an oxygen tank on top, but a number painted to be seen from above.

There were six lines of traffic, with two open lanes between each of them. Lisa recognized the Bulldog on the few Mack trucks. The remaining types of semi-trucks she'd never heard of, but she'd never heard of a Freightliner a week ago, so that wasn't saying much. All the trucks were big, gas or diesel powered, and all were hauling trailers. Lisa looked back down the tarmac. Actually, most of the big rigs were hauling two or more trailers; two giant semi trucks pulled in with four full trailers each. But every truck, RV, bus or trailer had the same large extended steel bumpers with huge rubber covers, and between each trailer were similar bumpers.

If this is a murder plan, it is ridiculously complicated.

"How you doing?" A man asked.

Lisa startled and turned to the young man who had spoken to her.

"Hi, I'm Jim, one of the coordinators."

She shook the hand he offered. *When was the last time someone offered me their hand?*

Jim was smiling. "It's important that you stay close to your vehicle. Is this your first time?"

"Um, yes. I'm Lisa, the blue Freightliner," she pointed down the line.

"Oh, Rick, yeah, good driver. He's done this longer than I have." Jim smiled. "I'm working for land on – oh, look at the countdown – have to get the livestock covered. Ah, Lisa was it, yeah you need to get to your truck. It's almost time." His mouth was a line as he turned and hurried to the nearest trailer.

Lisa looked up at the overhead signs. They were like what you'd find at a racetrack or interstate highway but repeated down the pre-trip staging area maybe every fifty feet, she wasn't sure, but a little closer than streetlights, maybe. And they were pointed down, so you just had to look up and see the indicated lanes, messages, and the timers.

Not that it was hard to miss the lanes. The black tarmac had white painted lines and yellow safety parking lanes. The paint looked fresh. Lisa looked closer, it had been painted repeatedly. She looked up. The count down hit the five-minute mark and the colour on the whole sign – all the signs, changed from green to yellow. A woman's voice came over the loud speakers, "T minus five minutes. Get them covered. All engines should be running. We have connection. We have connection."

The noise level dropped as people jumped, ran, or hurried about.

Lisa froze, *if this is so cool why is everyone suddenly so quiet?*

The woman's voice came again, "Connection is good, repeat connection is solid."

People cheered. Horns were honked and the excitement level jumped. The horses vanished behind the rubber cover.

"Lisa!" Brian, her boyfriend of five years, husband of a week, called from next to the Freightliner. "Lisa! Come on." He waved her forward.

She picked up her pace toward the waiting truck, as Brian glanced about at the people like them, and yet not. There were families, children were crying, young people in groups, old people too, and a lot of couples. She noticed more and more groups of young men on their own. A large commercial bus filled with people was loading backpacks and boxes to her right, the top of the bus was covered with a tarp, it was a good four feet high with who knew what, and it was pulling a long narrow trailer. Several large RVs began filling in the gaps between the trucks, most pulling their own various sized trailers. A long body older truck cartoonishly loaded down with stuff, pulling a huge RV honked and she darted out of the way. All the livestock trailers were now covered by rubberized tarps. Almost every vehicle but the semis had stuff piled on top of it, as if an extra box or plastic container or bag might be the difference between survival or failure.

Overhead the woman's voice came, "T minus two minutes. Contact is solid. All systems are green. We are a go! We are a go!"

Brian hurried toward her. “You have a conference call. If you’re keeping the phone it has to go into the bag, Lisa! Come on.”

“I know.” She took her phone. Its screen had four tiny faces in three squares. Turning it, they were bigger. Her sister, Kimber, was waving, gesticulating from her own phone; her brother David was smiling from his bedroom, and gave her a wave; her parents were together in their kitchen. As Brian tugged her along, she tapped the mute.

“Stop, Lisa! Don’t be a colonizer!” Kimber yelled.

Brian snapped, “For fuck sakes! How stupid is she!”

“You’re forcing my sister with your white male privilege!”

Lisa hit the mute on her sister’s image, as she and her parents said, “Shut up, Kimber!”

“Lisa, listen to me,” her mother said through tears. “There is no infrastructure. Do you hear me? They admitted it on TV. No infrastructure!”

Her father nodded. “No power, no running water, hell, no clean water!”

“I know. We know.”

David, her eighteen-year-old brother had yet to say anything.

They were at the truck now. Brian held open the passenger door and she climbed in. The passenger seat was big, but it would be tight. Rita offered to let her sit behind the passenger seat. Brian sat down and she squeezed in beside him.

“I want to sit with Brian,” Lisa shifted. “Just in case this trip fails.”

Her mother burst into loud sobs.

“The news says they’re lying!” her dad yelled. “Think about it! It’s impossible!”

Rita, the driver's wife, was sitting behind Rick, the driver, she smiled encouragingly but gave a big sigh.

Brian cranked the window open.

"Please, don't do this, sweetie!" Her mom leaned into the phone; face wet. "Even if it's true, if something goes wrong there will be no one to help you! Don't you understand? No one."

"Lisa, listen to your mother." Her father's face seemed older than when she'd seen him three days ago. "You won't even be able to return for five years. Or get us a message."

"That isn't true, it'll just be hard."

"There aren't any hospitals, sweetie. What happens if...if...any thing happens? You could die from an infection! From a scratch!"

"Mom, Dad, I love you both. I love all of you. But we're doing this."

Her dad looked a bit wild. Then he leaned in, "Brian, please!"

"I'll do my best to look after her, sir. My absolute best."

They were moving. Lisa looked up but she could only see the trailer in front of them.

"You could die just trying to get there!" Her mother was sobbing.

Kimber's voice was loud as she came through the kitchen door behind their parents. She was yelling about colonizing, waving a baseball bat.

Brian yelled, "Phillip! Behind you!"

Lisa gasped. Her hand clutched Brian's. "Oh, god!

Through the small screen, she saw her dad grab the bat and shoved Kimber hard. He was yelling at her, demanding to know what was wrong with her.

"Mom, please, kick Kimber out! She is stupid, dangerously stupid. She is going to kill you, both of you, or leave you sick and homeless. What about David? Do you want him on the street?"

"Don't say that. She's just confused."

"Marlene, she doesn't—she can't think. She doesn't understand anything. For god's sake Marlene, she tried to feed us all rotten chicken. We could have died."

Marlene picked up her phone. "That's why you have to stay! You have to come home. We need your help."

"No mom," Lisa wiped at her own tears. "No, mom. Brian's right. She won't listen to you, or anyone. Kick her out, mom."

Dad reappeared, "I've locked her outside."

"I love you both. I love you, David, and I love Kimber, too. But we need a future, and there isn't one here."

David waved at her, tears in his eyes. "I wish I was going with you."

Now both her parents were crying.

"I have to put the phone away. I'll get you a message, and it won't take five years. I love you all. Wish us luck."

David was the only one who did.

Over the intercom and the radio, the woman's voice informed everyone that electronic devices had to be shielded in thirty seconds. Turning off the phone, Lisa slipped it into the Faraday bag and sealed it.

"They'll be okay." Brian put his arm around her.

Lisa realized that the woman from the loud speaker, was on the radio.

"Look at them idiots," Rick the driver said, motioning through the passenger window.

Looking out through the break between the truck and trailer next to them, she saw the huge double fence. Hundreds of people were hitting the outer one, yelling, and waving signs.

"When she hits zero," said Rita from the back seat, "they're going to get a shock. I mean that literally."

Everyone was counting, she could hear it over the yelling. *Five. Four. Three. Two. One.*

Screams came from the crowd. People had fallen. Some were struggling to get up or were stumbling around. But there had been no flash, nothing.

Radio: *"Connection is solid. We are green...We are go. Repeat, we are go. Keep drop out lanes open. Roll to ten."*

"What—" Lisa started as Rick put the truck into gear.

"Windows up, Brian, please," Rita said handing Lisa two small, compressed air canisters connected to a plastic mask like on airplanes. "You don't have to put it on dear, but just like in training, please hang it around your neck. And remember, just like on a plane you put it on yourself first, same with you, Brian. We can't help anyone if we're unconscious."

Brian turned the window crank as the woman's voice on the radio said, fifteen.

Rita squeezed Lisa's arm. "You don't worry about them, dear. And I'm sure you sister will be okay. Young people can be very passionate, but once she gets a little older, she'll start thinking more."

Brian snorted. "She's twenty-eight."

"Oh," Rita sat back. "Well, your brother seems nice?"

"Yeah, David is. He's trying to get off his meds so he can come. He's been on anxiety and depression meds for years. He's only seventeen." Lisa wiped at the tears. "At least Brian's family is positive."

Huge airships, dirigibles they'd been called in training, were flying ahead, but she couldn't see much with the trucks and trailers around them.

The woman on the radio said, *"We have radio connection. We are green. Twenty."*

"Yes," Rita said, gripping her husband's shoulder.

"Time to focus people," Rick said.

Radio: *"Twenty-five."*

"That's our speed?" Brian asked.

"Yes," Rick said. "When we enter the wormhole, we're going to be doing one hundred miles an hour."

"Why so fast?" Lisa saw that there were fewer people along the fences. Most were looking at their dead phones and not the trucks speeding by. Then the trailer cut off her view.

"Yeah, shouldn't we go slow and careful?"

"Hell, no." Rick barked a laugh. "Faster we go the more people get through. We don't want to be stuck in the middle—"

"Or near the beginning," Rita cut in.

"You're right, babe," Rick said, glancing at the vehicles around them. The woman on the radio said thirty-five and Rick increased their speed in unison with everyone else. "That would be worse, you can't exactly turn around fast in these rigs."

"But they leave the two lanes on the edges for turnaround?" Brian asked peering up through the window.

The woman said, *"Journey time today is ninety-seven minutes. Journey time today is ninety-seven minutes. Forty."*

"Oh, don't like that," Rita said squeezing Rick's shoulder.

"We'll be fine."

"Sorry, I hate anything over an hour," Rita sighed.

"So, a minute might be a light year?" Brian asked.

"Can be." Rita shrugged. "Can be more, usually is."

"It's the route that's picked," Rick said. "Depends on the connections made. If it goes one side of any of the seven black holes or the other, that changes the distance, and the power."

"Yeah, that seems really confusing." Lisa peered up at the signs, forty-five appeared even as the radio announced the speed change.

"Oh, people far smarter than us are scratching their heads every time one of these things connects," Rick laughed. "I just drive my truck here; she keeps us safe and moving."

"Fifty."

"Shit," Rick said as they passed a truck that had pulled into one of the stopping lanes.

"They're not going?" Brian asked looking back but the truck was past.

"Don't know. Might be a mechanical problem, or people changing their minds." Rick geared up as fifty-five was announced.

They heard an old school radio crackle, full of static, from behind as Rita asked what was going on. A man's voice said something that Lisa didn't catch. Sixty was announced

Rita was back between the seats. "Ain't that a thing. Rodney had a pickup. Apparently, his ride's wife changed her mind and is coming."

Rick shook his head. "Love's a thing but we only got till seventy-five for anyone to change their minds."

Radio: *"Sixty-five."*

"I was told we could change our minds right up to the – the opening?" Lisa asked.

"Technically, yes," Rita said, "but it messes things up. Did have it happen a few times, though. And if you're planning on changing your mind, could you do it now?"

Brian looked at Lisa, his face full of concern. "I'm not forcing you. If you don't want to go, we're not going."

Love filled Lisa, it stopped the tears, and she tightened her hands on her husband's. "We're going. We're modern settlers and we have ten times more knowledge, understanding, heck, more stuff for survival than they did. They made it. We're going to make it."

Brian crushed her to him as seventy was announced.

They were coming around now to where they had parked earlier. Lisa peered out the window.

Over the radio the woman said, "If you're pulling out, now is the time, boys and girls. You have this lap only."

Lisa swallowed. There were still people scattered on the other side of the fence, but most were sitting down or watching, some appeared to be laying down.

"Sad. Some of them kids have never been without their phones since they were babies," Rita said. "Now their phones and all it's data is gone, wiped by the EMP."

"Oh," Lisa wondered how that was going to be for them. She tried to imagine Kimber without her phone and couldn't. But was she any different even with weeks offline? *I'm bringing mine even though there is no connection on Nova Terra, no phone services, no medical services...no roads.* "How do we get anywhere?"

"You mean on Nova?" Rick asked.

"Yeah, yes." Brian nodded. "I've been wondering."

"Well, there's the airships, rivers, and ridges." Rick said. "We're entering at site fourteen this trip."

"They announced it over the radio," Rita said. "Just after connection."

"That's a ridge site. Would have preferred site 8 or 9," Rick said. "That would have put us close to home."

"Home?" Brian and Lisa asked together.

Rita smiled. "We have ourselves a place on Lake Ednora, named after our kids."

"You got to name it?" Lisa asked.

"Sweetie they're dead worlds, I mean they're Earth-like, gravity, and everything, but until two years ago the oxygen was too low to live comfortably—didn't you take the intro?"

"Yes, but...it seems impossible..." Brian started.

"Two years? How is that possible?" Lisa asked.

"Seventy-five."

Rick asked, "We going?"

Rita looked at Lisa and Brian. They both nodded.

"Need to hear it," Rick said.

"Yes," Lisa said looking at Brian.

He looked down at her and nodded. "Yes."

Rick flashed his lights and picked up speed.

"Eighty."

"They've been planting plants all over the planet," Rita said. "All the planets. And there's something in the ocean, some plant from Earth that has oxygen as a waste product, and they spread it everywhere. And of course, plankton, both the animal and plant kind is spread everywhere. And they're planting kelp, and other water plants." Rita sighed. "No fish yet, but next year they're bringing whales."

"How?" Lisa blinked trying to listen to instructions on the radio about groups closing up.

"Big tanker has one of whose trucks from the oil fields pulling it," Rick spoke with awe in his voice.

"I think she means how is the poor things going to live, Rick," Rita said. "They are raising fish along the shore right now and in dugouts. They'll have enough to feed them. And the whales have volunteered so that's okay."

"Wait, what?" Brian blinked.

"Oh, yeah, you weren't supposed to give that away, Babe."

"Eighty-five."

"They've been able to talk to whales for years. Cured cancer, too." Rita's voice had a sudden edge, and her mouth had become a line. "Bastards let us lose our Elizabeth because cancer generates profits and controls populations. In the nineteen-eighties they had shots for most cancers; been fighting the cures coming out for decades. Fuck them and their profits."

"Rita!" Rick admonished. "Babe, I hate'em too, but they are not winning, woman. Not winning. Their wealth is collapsing. They're backstabbing each other. Their greed is their demise. They are going to jail. Natural law."

"I can't forgive." Rita leaned onto her husband's shoulder, her hand on his shoulder.

"I love you," Rick said.

Lisa looked away, leaning into Brian. His arms tightened around her.

"Ninety. Group twenty-seven time to close up."

"That's us," Rick said.

Rita sat back.

As they turned, Lisa saw that they were no longer on the loop, now they were following their lane in and the two empty lanes on either side were filled as the trucks and trailers closed in.

"One hundred. Repeat, one hundred. May whatever Gods you believe in aide your journey; good luck to all of you! Our hopes and dreams go with you. First line entering in five."

Lisa leaned forward. They were getting closer to the truck in front—would she miss it?

"Four."

They were on the straightaway. Heading for what looked like the entrance to a giant tunnel.

"Three".

A tunnel that went nowhere, it was too short. The tunnel was thirty feet deep.

"Two."

And they were heading toward it at a hundred miles an hour.

The black maw appeared between the vehicles in front.

"One".

We are going to die!

She caught a glimpse of the dirigible floating outside the entrance, a cable hanging from it going into the tunnel—A wall of white mist swallowed those in front.

Then they were through. Breathing hard, heart pounding – the sun was gone. They were driving under a weird night sky, all distorted and streaky.

"...this is your Starlight Express. Again, my name is Amanda for all of you just entering. You are flying through the void, far faster than the speed of light."

"Oh, I like her," Rita said. "She plays the good rock music."

"They've given me this book of about three hundred pages explaining the tech that is allowing you to drive across the stars to another arm of the Milky way. I don't care. If you're interested, you can get your own copy on the other side. Welcome to the Starlight Express. I'm one hundred and twenty feet above you all, floating in an air ship, millions and millions of miles from Georgia. Ain't life funny. And none of us is ever going to be the same." Louie Louie, by the Kingsmen started playing.

Brian laughed. It sounded a bit off to Lisa.

"You okay, love? Brian?"

"We're travelling to another arm of the Milky Way, to a planet whose intelligent species wiped themselves out about six million years ago, and we're doing it in a nineteen-nineties semi truck listening to sixties rock, while travelling faster than the speed of light." He rubbed his face with his hands.

"Have some tea, Brian. It has milk and sugar." Rita poured from a thermos into a plastic cup.

Brian looked at her, blinking. "Tea?"

"It really will make everything better." Rita handed the cup to Brian who stared at it.

Lisa took then pushed the cup into her husband's hand. "Brian, love, drink it."

"Do you want some, Lisa?"

"Yes, please." Lisa pushed Brian's hand until the cup met his lips. "Are you okay?"

"It's just...the lady on the radio...Amanda...she's right, nothing is ever going to be the same."

Lisa took the cup that Rita offered, then looked into Brian's eyes. "It's like you said, we're on a wagon train to literally a new world.

"Riiiick," Rita cautioned.

"Sorry, but we're not the wagons. Brian, think about it." Rick glanced over.

Brian took a sip of tea and stared at Rick, hard. On the radio Runaway, sung by Del Shannon started playing.

"We're the ships, Brian. Think about it. If there was bad weather or whatever half those ships didn't make it. And when they did, if half the passengers made it, they were happy. Some were so bad they called them coffin ships."

Brian's face went pale.

Lisa glared at Rick. *Oh, no, it's all true.*

"Already, we're bucking the odds, son. Ninety-nine point nine are making it, Brian. We're already doing better."

"We're going to make it?"

"Maybe." Rick watched the road. "The only thing that really matters, Brian, is that woman in your arms. You could have died this morning on the toilet. You could have died on your way to the staging area."

On the radio, the Beach Boys sang about their Little Deuce Coupe.

"You're on the ship, right now son. We still got to make to that distant shore. I'll have a cup of tea, Babe."

Rita poured another cup and handed it to Rick.

There was dead air on the radio, then Amanda cut in, *"A bit of choppy weather up ahead, people. We got some bounce coming up, so stay focused. So far, we're still green."* Aretha Franklin belted Respect.

Rita handed them each a sick bag.

"We're still on the ship."

"That's right, son, and Lisa needs you to hold it together." Rick took a sip. "You ain't going to Nova for the climate, ain't for the fishing either. You are going so that the two of you can start a family. You're going to build a new world. And we'll get to those shores."

"Or die trying?" Brian asked.

"Or die trying," Rick nodded.

Perry Como started to sing about how Papa Loves Mambo. The truck ahead dipped.

"What's happening?" Lisa leaned tight into Brian.

"Like turbulence, dear," Rita said. "Maybe we should put our seat belts on. I always feel for the poor cows when this happens."

Little Eva sang The Locomotion.

Rita sang along. Then came the Big Bopper, singing Chantilly Lace, and it turned out that Rick had a pretty good voice.

Sloopy was being asked to hang on by the McCoys, as the road rose and fell. The tea had felt good but now, Lisa's stomach was starting to revolt.

Outside the stars were growing brighter and seemed to be moving in weird ways, sometimes speeding up, then slowing, then zipping away.

Elvis was All Shook Up, when Lisa suddenly felt light.

"Better get our seat belts on." Rita tapped Lisa's shoulder. "Did you hear me, Brian? Lisa, if you want you can sit back here with me?"

Brian shook his head; his arms were tight around Lisa.

"Let's buckle up."

Through the windshield the universe above them was filled with light and movement. Ice formed on the window. "Um, is that supposed to happen?" Lisa asked.

"We appear to have sprung a leak, people, but you're almost through, and people up here are tapping away at buttons. Don't hold your breath. And remember me, and your Starlight drive when you go out into the light." Mustang Sally, sung by Wilson Pickett played next.

Lisa found herself held down by the seat belt as they dropped down another rise. *What was that?* "Did you see that?" Stars were suddenly shooting across the sky.

Rita gripped Rick's shoulder.

Lisa was getting lighter and lighter.

"The other reason we use old trucks is that they're heavy," Rita said. "And stick to the road."

"But it's not a real road, it's whatever the wormhole..." Brian paled.

"Brian, don't be taking it apart in your head."

"But we don't know how it works! The Aliens that are letting us use this – their—":

"Do you know how your cell phone works, I mean beyond the basics?"

"No, but it's not the same!"

"Brian, its exactly the same," Rick said "I know that in this wormhole is a highway. I know I'm a trucker, and we all know we're in a convoy." Rick blew the air horn.

Others began honking.

Amanda came on, "*Guess it's time.*"

Lisa glanced on the radio. *Time for what?*

C.W. McCall started the Convoy song. Brian laughed.

When the verse came up, instead of singing across the USA, Rita yelled, '...Across the Milky Way!"

The song was just finishing when Amanda cut it and said, *"Blow out ahead of truck 44, that's Rick and Rita, truck 44—we've got sabotage, people! Sabotage! Rick, Denny, Martha, Jim-Boy, tighten up! Tighten up!"*

Rita gasped. "Damn it."

"What does she—" Brian was cut off as the truck slammed into the one in front.

Far from slowing down, Rick pressed the gas pedal.

"What?" Lisa gripped Brian's hand.

"We can't stop, Lisa." Rita's hand gripped Lisa's shoulder. "Someone in the truck ahead of us might have killed Frankie."

"John is with him," Rick said, face hard and pale.

Brian looked from the truck in front, to Rick. "Who's John?"

"Frankie's grandson." Rita's voice was filled with pain. "He's taking over the truck next month. I hope that kid's okay."

"Sabotage?" Lisa felt the truck buck. The bumpers made sense as the Freightliner's bumper connected with the one in front.

"We can't stop and can't slow down." Rita was back on her radio.

Sudden weight pushed Lisa into her seat. Brian moaned.

"Gravity's back on," Rick said.

Suddenly the truck in front pulled away.

Amanda was back on the radio, *"Good news, Frankie's ride-a-long, and passengers saved the day. Frankie will be pulling off just after the opening. It's ten in the morning, local time, bright and sunny. If you have sunglasses I recommend them. And here's a song for the idiot."* Folsom Prison Blues, sung by Johnny Cash, filled the cab.

Lisa saw a flash of light, the 'hills' were flattening out and then were gone.

The white half circle was getting closer and bigger.

"What's that?" Brian asked.

"That, son, is Nova Terra, get ready, because tonight you won't recognize any of the stars in the sky." Rick smiled.

"It's the weirdest thing, it really is the thing that will weird you out the most," Rita added.

Brian gave a laugh, it was mostly a good laugh, only crazy on the edges.

"So, we're still on the ship?" Brian asked.

"And we're about to make landfall."

Lisa leaned forward as the white half circle grew larger and larger and then they were through it. She gasped as they drove over a little bump and then were driving down a rough ramp onto packed earth. The light was blinding, and she blinked tears as she squinted. Around her, Nova Terra was shades of off white and dusty. They drove for twenty minutes before a guy standing in the back of a pickup truck motioned them to the right. They pulled up and stopped.

Opening the door, Brian got out first and helped Lisa down. The air was cold, dry, dusty, smelling like a hot summer day in the city, but thin like mountain air. The morning sun lacked heat but filled the world with golden light.

"We're here, Lisa."

She looked up at her man. "Yeah. We are."

Looking back, Lisa saw a metal frame and heavy black wire attached to the half circle where weird balls floated, the opening to the wormhole was a black portal lit by emerging headlights and streaky stars, that eight lines of trucks and trailers poured out of.

She looked up, Brian was sweating, face white, he wasn't looking at the trucks and trailers pouring out, filling the air with dust. He was looking at the horizon opposite the morning sun. Lisa looked. Instead of one moon, there was two: one full, and one a partial fingernail.

Reaching up, she tugged his gaze to her. "We're here. We made it to shore."

He nodded, holding her tight. "Yeah. We did."

"Now to get our wagon and land."

Brian smiled. "Yeah."

Together they turned to look where the vehicles were vanishing in clouds of dust as they drove off. Ahead of them was a whole new world.

The End

Gemstone: Part One

Lasalina Tess

Chimes jingle as I open the door to Jacob's Trading, and I'm struck by the welcoming scent of incense and minerals. Shelves of various stones fill the small store, along with boxes of tarot cards, figurines, jewellery, and other tiny treasures. A woman scolds three children, who touched things they shouldn't have. One takes off running, squealing in delight toward a bin of brightly coloured beads. The pitch is deafening. I grasp my necklace and slip a finger between the cage rings to touch my anxiety stone.

"Tara, you're back!" A familiar male voice says.

I smile. "Hi, Matt. Busy day?"

He rolls his eyes and gestures at the noisy family running through the aisle. "You could say that."

Kids are not in my near future, and I'm okay with that. "Did they come in yet?" I lean against the front counter, watching him write in a ringed notebook.

"Sure did! I just finished setting them up." Matt drops his pen and walks out from behind the counter. "Follow me."

At least this time it wasn't pointless stopping by on my way home from work. I should have called ahead of time, but being a last-minute decision while driving, it didn't occur to me earlier. We reach the back corner of the store where Mike stops in front of a shelf.

"Here they are, fresh off the truck." A clatter echoes through the store, startling us. "Excuse me, Tara," Matt says, hurrying away.

I struggle to hold my laughter. "Thanks, Matt." I'm glad I'm not the one dealing with that. Who would bring young children into a store that carries breakables? At least the rocks are safe. The rock castle model is the same one I have at home, only in better condition, and this one carries at least ten dragon figurines. In front of it are even more dragons, each painted in beautiful colours: purple, red, gold, green, and blue. Beneath the store's lighting, they glimmer and sparkle, as if the designers were attempting to mimic magic. Some hover protectively over eggs or gemstones, while others spread their wings like they are about to take off. They will make a magical addition to my fantasy collection that sits in my home office, right above my high fantasy novels. If only I could buy all of them at once.

One by one, I pick each of them up to inspect its design, inhaling the fresh-off-the-shelf scent. I'll buy three today, and another three in two weeks, provided they haven't sold out by then. Maybe Matt would tuck some aside for me. A beautiful purple dragon catches my eye. In its talons is a yellow gemstone in a gold setting. If it were genuine gold, it would cost more than I can afford. I reach for it, but a red glimmer reflects off my glasses, interrupting my field of view. Sitting on the top tier of the castle is a translucent red stone unlike any that the dragons carry. The surface appears unpolished, but inside, it glows red. Maybe it's catching light from somewhere in the store.

A child screams, "No!"

The mother says firmly, "We are leaving. Now!"

There it is, that moment where she learns her lesson. I glance over my shoulder but can't see anyone through the over-crowded shelves. If I had children, this would be the last place I would take them. Refocusing on the shelf in front of me, I reach for the strange red stone. As I touch it, warmth shoots through my arm, and I pull away. The stone isn't connected to electricity; I've been here many times and there's never been any cords connecting to the castle. With a deep breath, I try again, this time picking it straight up from the castle. This time, heat surges through my body, and I gasp for breath. My vision darkens like I'm about to pass out, and I clutch the shelf for support. The room seems to spin, and my balance wavers.

Darkness surrounds me as I fall.

A fluttering in my ear rouses me. A bug? I wave my hand around, shooing whatever it is away. When it stops, I lay my arms back down on the floor. Only it's not the floor, it's cool grass. I open my eyes to stare up at a star-filled sky. How long have I been out for? Where am I?

My head spirals as I sit up. I'm in a clearing surrounded by trees. The scent of wildflowers and grass tickles my nose, making me sneeze. Large butterflies are everywhere, landing on flowers or fluttering around each other like a dance. How did I get here? I never knew there was a place like this in Winnipeg. Maybe I'm in one of the provincial parks.

I stand to look around. The only lights are from bugs that glow from time to time, on and off like adjustable smart bulbs. Fireflies. Which way is the parking lot? Everywhere I look is dark. I'm in the middle of a forest. My heart thunders in my chest, and I grip my anxiety stone necklace, eager to find calm and figure out what happened. My phone. I reach for my purse, but it's no longer on my shoulder. I drop to my knees, dragging my hands through the grass, but find nothing.

A strong breeze gusts through my hair, and a loud sound whooshes overhead like a bird flying. Its dark silhouette blocks out the stars, casting a shadow over the entire clearing. That's too big to be a bird. Adrenaline fills my core, and without another thought, I dart toward the trees. Whatever that flying creature is, I have no desire to meet it. The grass is so tall that it reaches my waist, forcing me to leap like a deer to gain any ground.

Five feet from the nearest tree, there's an enormous boom and the ground beneath me trembles, sending me rolling the rest of the way. My body slams into the thick tree trunk, leaving me breathless. Pain sears through my back, and my heart pounds in my ears.

Tremors continue through the ground in a steady rhythm. When it finally stops, a wave of heat flows over me as if someone flicked on a portable heater. All I can see is darkness. What was that? Head throbbing, I force myself to sit, leaning back against the tree.

Purple globes float down from the treetops, emanating in the darkness. My gaze focuses on them. They're like balloons that glow in the dark. Only these have black narrow slits through their centre that are narrow at the top and bottom, yet thicker in the middle. Almost like cat's eyes.

Eyes.

A shock of numbness rushes through my limbs, reaching my head.

All consciousness leaves me.

Crackling and the scent of campfire smoke rouse me. The aching in my back is worse than before, spreading all the way up my neck. Yet I'm not lying against the tree any longer. Soft fur tickles my hand, and I'm so warm that I could break out in a sweat any moment. Purple globe-like eyes haunt my thoughts. Tense, I open my eyes and shoot upright. What happened? Who moved me?

Flames dance upon logs that are circled by three large rocks. Light flickers, offering a small glimpse of my surroundings. Beneath me is a long stretch of grey fur in the shape of what once must have been a wolf. Its musky smell blends with smoke. The scent is intense, but not intense enough to make me ill. This can't be real. Moments ago, I was picking out dragons at Jacob's Trading. Now, I'm in the woods with a random campfire, lying on top of a dead wolf's pelt. Beyond the immediate area, I see nothing.

With the light of the fire, it makes the forest darker. Thankfully, I cannot see those creepy floating cat-eyes.

Pulling my knees tight against my chest, I hug them, replaying events in my mind. Everything changed the moment I touched that stone on the rock castle. Was it poisonous? Has someone abducted me and taken me for a ride to the woods? It doesn't make any sense. How can I not remember how I got here?

Heavy breathing sends a chill down my spine. Gooseflesh spreads across my arms. I don't want to look. I don't want to see who's watching me. Or what? I can sense the creature nearby, lurking in the darkness. Its hot breath creates distortion on the other side of the fire. Purple eyes appear, smaller than before thanks to their distance from me. I hug my knees even tighter, trying to make myself smaller and hopefully less visible. Wake up, Tara!

A thump pulls my gaze to the right of the fire, where four logs hit the ground and roll a bit before coming to a stop. Next to them is a pair of legs. Brown leather pants topped with a toned, bare abdomen between the edges of an open leather vest. Broad shoulders. Muscular arms.

"It's okay," the male voice says.

I loosen the grip on my knees and position myself for a better look.

Stubble lightly coats the man's face. His jawline is strong, as are his cheekbones. Thick brown eyebrows match his hair, which stands up about four inches high in the front and settles three inches shorter in the back. The strangest thing about this man is the unique shape of his ears. They start out normal against his head, but stick out a bit too much, reaching a point near the top of his head.

One corner of his lip curves upward. "This must be a lot to take in," he says. "It usually is when someone first comes through a portal."

"A what?" I say, my voice quiet, almost unfamiliar.

The man kneels on the ground and slides another log onto the fire. "A portal," he continues. "Between your world and this one."

Laughter escapes me. This guy must be on drugs. Portals and other worlds? Or maybe I'm the one on drugs. Those purple eyes keep re-appearing in the distance. "What is that?" I say, staring at the obscured creature through the flames.

The man's gaze follows mine, then returns to focus on me. "We'll get to that soon enough," he says. "Maybe try to relax a bit, take some time to adjust."

Why won't he just answer my question? "Who are you?"

"My friends call me Roan, and you may also," he answers. "And you?"

"Tara." A stray strand of brown hair drifts across my face, so I tuck it behind my ear.

Roan pokes the fire with a long stick, sending embers floating above. "And you are human?"

"What else would I be?"

He glances at me. "I did not intend to offend you, Tara, but I've often wondered if portals would open to other worlds, aside from Earth."

Earth. Yes, that's where I'm from. So, if I'm no longer on my planet, where am I?

As though reading my thoughts, Roan says, "We are in Calidora, between the Elf Queen's city and the Dragon King's mountain-home." He stands and walks along the fire's side, watching the flames dance as he speaks. "Long ago, a young female Guarri named Taelina broke the rules of her people and tapped into an ancient magic that opened a portal. This forbidden portal linked our worlds together. Soon after, humans arrived, one after another, until an entire village worth, had no choice but to settle in Calidora."

If this is true, then there are more of us nearby. Maybe they can help make sense of this. "Why didn't they just return through the portal? Isn't it a doorway that you can walk through from either side?" At least that's how it worked in The Chronicles of Narnia.

With a sigh, he nears and sits cross-legged in front of me, gaze intense. "Unfortunately, this is not the case. Taelina did not understand the strength of the magic she used and therefore created a one-way portal. Those who arrived can never return through it."

"So, I'm trapped here?" My heart rate quickens, reality striking me like a bowling ball to the head.

Roan sighs. "Yes, I'm sorry. I can't imagine how you must be feeling. There are ways of returning, but it is rare to find hidden portal stones. They are buried deep within the mountains of Calidora, protected by the dwarfs and dragon king."

Hope reaches my heart like a warm gust of air. "Will you help me find one?" Wait, did he say dragon king?

His eyes widen, and the corner of his lip twitches as if a smile hesitates to emerge. "Even if we gained access to the caves, dwarves are unlikely to trade with humans, and you have nothing to trade." Roan stands and shakes his head. "Then it must be taken to the Guarri cave-home to be connected with the original portal, which could only be accomplished by the Guarri master."

All hope, little though there is, fades, leaving a weight on my chest. "What you're saying is... it's impossible."

He folds his arms across his chest and taps his foot on the ground. "If it were possible to strike an agreement with the dwarfs, surely humans would have done so by now. Allow me time to think about this."

To be trapped in this unknown world, with no chance of returning home, is terrifying. What creatures and dangers will I encounter? Can this guy be trusted? Maybe someone else here knows more and has a way back to Earth. Everything inside me screams that this is not a dream. All I can do is sleep and pray that when I wake up, I'll be back on the floor of Jacob's Trading in Winnipeg, Manitoba.

Hot air suffocates me, forcing me awake. I shield my face and struggle to find the cause. Did the fire spread? Large, purple, snake-like eyes hover over me. A massive set of nostrils huffs, sending steam into the morning air. My body numbs, fear holding me in place. The scream that swells in my throat refuses to escape.

"Talon, no!" Roan shouts. "You'll scare her!"

The dark blue and black scaled beast growls and steps away from me.

My voice trembles as I'm finally able to speak. "What... is that?" Deep down, I know what it is. I've spent most of my life dreaming about them. Figurines line my bookshelf, representing what doesn't exist. And yet, here is the mystical creature, breathing nearby, filling me with dread. What if fire flies from the dragon's mouth, consuming everything in its path? Is he hungry, and will I be his next meal?

"It's alright," Roan assures me, as he reaches my side. "Talon is a dragon I've known since her birth. She will not harm you, I promise."

Each of my limbs shakes from the adrenaline coursing through my body. Never in my life could I have imagined this. Only in my dreams were dragons real. Until now.

Roan faces Talon and gestures to the ground. The dragon lowers herself across the dew-soaked grass and rests her head in a position to face me. Warm breath continues to flow, yet it's less intense. Her large purple eyes blink and stare at me as though waiting for a response.

Something in her gaze calms me. These are not the eyes of a scary beast that intends to rip apart my flesh. They represent a gentle being who wants to know me. To be my friend. Is that even possible? I don't believe any of this. First, dragons exist, and second, one wants to befriend me. Never mind having an obvious name like Talon. An insane laugh escapes my lips. I tap my cheeks with both hands, hoping it will either wake me up or confirm that this is real.

I'm not waking up.

Roan places a hand on Talon's large snout. "You can touch her if you'd like." He gestures toward his scaled friend with encouragement.

Unsettled, the last thing I want to try is standing, so I crawl slowly towards the beast, careful to move aside from the line of her hot breath. Hands trembling, I reach out and touch the cool scales near her nostrils. They are as hard as metal, and as smooth as silk.

Welcome, Tara of Earth, a deep female voice says in my mind.

I yank back my hand. "She just..."

"Spoke?" Roan says. "Yeah, she tends to do that."

"Can she understand me?" I return my hand to her snout.

"Yes," he replies.

A rattle comes from Talon's throat, like the purr of a lion on steroids.

"Hello, Talon." My voice is like a terrified little girl's. "It's... an honour to meet you..."

It is I who am honoured, Talon replies. *Humans have nothing to fear from me.* She closes her mystical eyes for a moment, releases a long breath, and her body sinks further into the ground like she's about to fall asleep.

Roan moves next to me, kneeling on the ground. "You are safe with us, Tara. We'll take you to the human village at daybreak, so that you are among your own kind."

It would make me feel a little better to see someone else from Earth, but deep down all I want is to go home. "I appreciate your help, but I would prefer you to help me find a way back to Earth."

With a sigh, he leans back against Talon and closes his eyes.

I'll take that as a no.

Rest now, small one, Talon says. *With the morning sun, hope may be instilled in Roan.*

A smile stretches across my face, and I whisper, "Thank you, Talon." I lie in the grass and shift so that my back is against Talon's face. With the heat from her breath warming the surrounding air, I fall asleep with ease.

The smell of bacon pulls me back to the land of the living. I open my eyes with a start, as Roan swings a handful of freshly cooked meat in front of my face.

"Time to face your new world, Tara," Roan says, a hint of playfulness in his tone.

It's a good thing I'm not one of those people who can't handle positive people first thing. "Is that bacon?" I say, sitting upright. It takes a lot of focus for me to ignore the bloodstains across Roan's clothing.

He blinks, puzzled, then says, "It's boar."

With a shrug, I reply, "Same thing." Except stronger in taste, I guess. Talon is no longer here; how did her movements not wake me? Taking the meat from Roan, I examine my surroundings. A fresh fire crackles in the pit, where the boar's body cooks on a long branch, but there's no sign of the dragon.

"She's getting her own breakfast," Roan says, as though reading my thoughts. "She was kind enough to feed us first, but we'll need to wait for the boar to cook before we leave for the village. It's almost done."

His words strike me with a blade of disappointment. So much for Talon convincing Roan to help me find a way home. He must not enjoy working with the dwarfs or Guarri. My stomach tightens. In my hand, the boar bacon reminds me of my growing hunger. I missed supper last night, back when I was home on Earth. What I wouldn't give for a cup of coffee right now. Or a breakfast sandwich from Tim Hortons.

The intense, wild flavour of bacon fills my mouth with juices I've never experienced before. My tastebuds tingle. I could get used to this. A large shadow blocks the surrounding sunlight, and I glance up to see Talon flying overhead. That is something I may never get used to seeing.

While I finish eating, Roan covers Talon's back with a thick leather blanket and straps, making the concoction resemble a saddle. A pang of realization strikes me. Does he expect me to ride that thing? Don't get me wrong, I've dreamt of riding a dragon, but there's a vast difference between a dream and reality. "Maybe we could walk," I say, approaching the pair.

Roan laughs. "Not possible. It's way too far." He tightens a strap around Talon's stomach. "Don't worry, I'll tie you down."

Talon's massive head comes closer, her long neck curved to reach me. *You will not fall off,* she says. *And even if you did, I would catch you. I'm quite fast, you know.* She snorts, sending my long, messy brown hair out behind me and stopping my breath for a moment.

Gee, that makes me feel better. I fold my arms across my chest. "And what we discussed?"

"What's that?" Roan asks, glancing over his shoulder.

"Nothing," I answer.

I have a plan, Talon says, and she looks away.

Roan pats the saddle setup and walks closer to me, a gentle smile on his face. "Are you ready to be the first human ever to ride a dragon?"

My heart rate thunders in my chest. "Not really," I say, gripping my anxiety stone necklace tight. Laughter escapes me, and I grab my hair while pacing back and forth. I must be insane to even attempt this.

"Do something for me," Roan says. He rests his hands on my arms, guiding them to my sides with a slight force. "Close your eyes."

"What? Why?" If I do, he'll probably jump me and tie me up, then force me onto his dragon.

He smiles and steps closer. "Tara, you don't know me, so you don't trust me. I get it." With the edge of his finger, he lifts my chin. "Look into my eyes."

His breath is warm on my face; the scent of fresh-cut grass blended with the subtle aroma of delicious boar bacon fills my nostrils. My gaze meets his; warm hazel eyes make my stomach flutter.

Roan moves even closer, our noses nearly touching. He whispers, "Take a deep breath." His hands slip into mine, our fingers entangled.

This is not something I would let any guy just... do to me, but there's something about Roan that makes me feel... safe. I take a deep breath and release it slowly, aware of Talon watching us intently.

Talon's voice enters my mind. *Allow yourself to melt into the moment of just being close to Roan. Feel his touch and lose yourself in his eyes.*

What is she, his fairy godmother? His matchmaker? Maybe this was the plan she was talking about last night.

Stay focused and breathe, Talon continues.

In Roan's eyes, I am drawn to the green that is more vibrant than I'd originally thought. There is no solid hazel colour around his pupils, but there's a blend of rich browns and a green as bright as the grass in this strange world. They are inhuman eyes. Yet, something else swims in their depths; something powerful. It's like there's a storm cloud on the verge of exploding into a downpour. Everything surrounding us fades away, and it's just Roan and I, linked. Warmth flows through my limbs, which fades to leave a tingling sensation. My heart rate calms. Fear disappears, becoming a small object in the back corner of my mind.

Every cell in my body feels as though it's being pulled toward Roan, trying to merge with the very fibre of his being. Should I be afraid? Is this man a threat? How is he doing this? All doubt suddenly vanishes, and I feel whole for the first time in my life.

The sensation suddenly fails as Roan pulls his hands from mine and steps back. His eyes are wide as he stares at me.

"What was that?" I ask him. "Is that... normal?"

Roan shakes his head. "Not quite." For a moment, he's quiet in thought. "Prolonged contact is used to improve connectivity between two friends, but never has it been so... intense."

I plant a hand firmly on my hip. "Were you trying to manipulate me?"

"Never," he replies. "It works how I explained; to strengthen the bond between friends. Never to manipulate or control another." Roan sighs. "I'm sorry if that made you uncomfortable."

"Whatever that was, it calmed my nerves, and it feels like we've known each other... forever." My cheeks flush. It isn't often I'm this open with someone. Especially someone I've only just met. Avoiding his gaze, I rub the newly formed gooseflesh on my arms.

"Are you cold?" Roan says.

"I wasn't before... but I am now..." Ever since he pulled away from me, a chill has spread throughout my body. It took time for me to notice, but it's as if someone has ripped my sleeping bag off me in the middle of the woods late at night, with no fire burning nearby.

Roan approaches Talon and flips open the latch on a large sack and then pulls out a large fur shawl-like item. “Take this,” he says, draping it over my shoulders. He pauses with his hands gripping the edges of the shawl, pulling it together beneath my chin. His voice is soft as he speaks. “It may be cool in the wind when we fly, but if you tuck in close to my back, it will help.”

All I can do is nod.

While I stand in a daze, Roan hurries along and packs up the cooked boar meat, then douses the fire and cleans up any remaining personal items. Then, with one gesture from Roan, Talon flattens herself along the grass while Roan helps me onto her back. One leg at a time, he straps me down, then jumps on in front of me.

Warmth fills me as I move in closer to his back, and even more so when he pulls my arms around his waist. A flutter of excitement dances in my stomach.

Roan glances over his shoulder, blinking, like he’s experiencing a similar sensation. “Ready?” he says.

I take a deep breath before answering, “Yes.”

The corner of his mouth curves upwards into a partial grin, then he faces ahead and pats the dragon’s shoulder.

Talon stands, sending a thrill through my body, like when a rollercoaster suddenly darts up a hill. Then her wings spread out, and she walks across the clearing to give herself space to extend them further. Without warning, a gust of wind pushes me downward, and my stomach flips as we climb into the Calidora sky. In a breath, we are past the trees, and for a moment I fear we’ll reach the clouds, but Talon levels off just above the forest.

In the distance to the right, which I believe is north, the land is higher and lined with mountains. We aren't high enough to see what lies beyond them. The forest stretches far ahead, and on the horizon to the left is the tallest mountain in the visible landscape.

Mount Calidora, Talon says. *Home to the great dragon king and the dwarves of the Wolf Clan.*

Ah yes, the species that is less than friend to us Earthlings, dwarves. And the location of a gemstone, if it exists, to return me home. If Roan decides to help me get there. If only I knew how to communicate with Talon.

I hear you, Earth child.

So, all I have to do is think, and she can hear me?

Instead of her voice entering my mind, she snorts, which is loud considering the volume of wind blowing in my ears.

My head throbs from the pressure of the wind, so I rest it against Roan's shoulder while I watch the wild land pass below. I've been to the countryside many times in my life, to go fishing and camping with my family, but nothing compares to this — hills and rock, valleys and dense forest. Dad would have loved this. Maybe not the ride itself, but the view. Mom, on the other hand, would have had to be dragged by the hair to venture this far into the wilderness. It's been five years since illness took them both. The pandemic changed everything.

Roan points to the North, and shouts, "That's one of the elf's cities!"

On the east side of the mountain, sunlight reflects off the tallest structure that reminds me of a Disney castle. It's difficult to see so far away, but the shape of it is clear enough that I can make out what it is. Living in such a beautiful place up there, far from reach, it must be so peaceful.

Seeing the land of Calidora from so high up is like a dream. What would it be like to stay here? There's so much to explore. And if that gemstone had magic, does that mean there's more? What if I get to the village and still feel like a stranger? Once I'm there, Roan and Talon will leave, and I may never see them again. A chill runs through me. I squeeze Roan tighter at the thought of losing this newfound connection.

His warm hand presses against mine, and our fingers interlock.

How can our bond be so strong, after only just meeting? I know nothing about him other than that he rides on the back of a dragon. Does he have someone else in his life who loves him? Could I fall in love with him myself? If he leaves me in the village, I'll never find out.

The edge of the forest comes into view, revealing planted crops and tiny figures labouring in the fields. Talon flies lower, and heads of the villagers tilt toward us. Children run along the grass, like they are trying to keep up with us; a playful game that reminds me of Earth. Past a row of wooden homes, Talon slows and then lands.

The world continues to spin around me, and I wait for my blood to stop rushing in my limbs.

An older gentleman jogs from the nearest building wearing suspenders and tan leather pants. "Greetings," he shouts. "I see you've brought us a new friend, Roan."

Roan chuckles. "That I have, Ben. This is Tara." His hand releases mine, and he shifts forward, preparing to dismount.

"Wait," I say. "Please."

Roan lifts his right leg over the saddle and shifts to face me. “Are you alright?” His words tell me one story, and his eyes tell me another. He nods and shouts, “Ben, will you give us a moment?”

Ben smiles and waves. “No worries. Come find me when you’re ready.” The farmer walks away, returning a straw hat to his head.

“What is it, Tara?” Roan moves his left leg over the saddle so that he is facing me head-on. “I need to hear you say the words, as I cannot read your mind like Talon can.”

With a deep breath, I glance at the foreign village with humans forced to survive here, with no hope of returning to Earth. It feels solitary, like it is for me back home. Sure, I have friends at work, but my family has either passed or moved far away. I meet Roan’s gaze and interlock our fingers to once again feel that intense sensation of being with him. “Roan, I want to stay with you.”

“What?” he says, eyes wide.

“At least, for as long as you’ll let me. We can get to know each other, and you can show me this amazing land of Calidora. Then, we can-”

Roan’s finger presses against my lips, stopping me. “You don’t have to say anything else.” He lowers his hand. “Whatever this is between us, I want to explore it.”

Without thinking, I throw my arms around him, pulling him against me.

Along my back, Roan’s gentle touch caresses me. “You were meant to find that stone,” he whispers. “Just like I was meant to find you.” He releases me, touches my face, then turns around to face forward in the saddle. Settling in, he calls out to a group of children hovering nearby, “Tell Ben we have changed our minds.”

Tiny faces look at each other with confusion, then back to us.

Feeling awkward, yet in a strange sense at peace, I wave to the human village, then hold on to Roan for takeoff.

To be continued...

Where Crusaders Walk

Trynda Adair

A tremble shook the pillars of the sanctuary, showering dust over his worn white tunic.

Amaury looked up towards the arched ceiling.

Cracks split the painted heavens overhead, threading through the gold stars. He followed the greatest of them as it reached toward the Madonna and Child set above the altar in silent vigil, stopping at the dark fold of her blue veil.

He let out the breath he held before making the sign of the cross.

"Where has young Amaury gone?" A gruff voice asked over another boom of landing trebuchet fire.

"Here, Messire," Amaury said, turning his back to the bare altar.

Standing next to a grey-haired priest clothed in dingy cream robes, was a knight adorned in chain mail and a similar white tunic with a red Cross of Jerusalem stitched into its chest.

"Bien. You are to accompany Sir Gérard —" the Lord Master pointed to another man with a shaved head and identical tunic adjusting his gauntlets, " — and escort Father Hugues with the most precious of cargo to safety."

"Oui, Seigneur," Amaury said with an obedient nod.

"Come before the altar for a blessing, my sons," the senior canon called stepping up from the Lord Master's side.

Knights lingering around the sanctuary gathered and knelt before the altar where Father Hugues stood as another volley shook the city.

A knot twisted in Amaury's stomach and he swallowed against the tightness in his throat. Was this the feeling within the sepulchre before Jerusalem fell? Is this how his uncle had spent his last hours?

"In nomine Patris, et Filii, et Spiritus Sancti. Amen." The men made the sign of the cross before the priest continued with the Our Father in Latin.

Another robed canon stepped forward, waiting with a bucket of holy water.

Father Hugues concluded the prayer and removed the sprinkler from the bucket. He stepped into the crowd of kneeling men, shaking the water over each knight as he spoke the next prayer.

"O King Almighty God, exercise the strength of your judgment, and order that we prevail over this ferocious people. O All-powerful Lord, through the fighting arm, restore to us the place of thy Holy Tomb, Amen."

After returning the sprinkler, the Senior Canon lifted a small reliquary holding a thumb-sized sliver of the cross where once Christ hung.

Amaury crossed himself as he gazed in awe at the relic.

The older priest made the sign of the cross with the reliquary as another volley of stones shook the cathedral.

"Go now, my sons, and may the Lord Almighty welcome you into his heavenly kingdom should you fall," Father Hugues said with a final sign of the cross.

At the other end of the Sanctuary, the rushed closing of heavy wood doors let out a soft, hollow thud. The sound of mail rushing and laboured breathing followed a slender-built knight as he rushed toward the commanding officers.

"Seigneur Maistre," the knight panted as he pulled the hot helmet from his head, "Seigneur Maistre, the walls of the city have been breached," The Lord Maistre looked to Sir Gerard with a nod before looking back to the young man gasping to catch his breath.

"Then we will make our stand in the house of the Lord, and give Gerard, Amaury, and Father Huges what time we can to see the True Cross to safety," The Lord Master spoke, looking across the cohort as he did.

He followed Sir Gérard, helmet in hand, falling into step behind the priest.

They headed down a side corridor before descending into a lower chapel.

"This symbol—" Gérard pointed to a small etched cross of Jerusalem,"—will show the way." Amaury nodded as they continued toward the catacomb entrance.

For a moment everything seemed to fall silent — then he heard it. The roar of stones thrown from a trebuchet.

He hesitated, awaiting the impact while Gérard wrestled with a key to open an ornate iron gate.

Bricks and dust exploded into the corridor as the stone collided with the cathedral.

He was thrown against the inner wall.

The breath forced from his chest.

Amaury's ears rang as he struggled to breathe, gasping like a fish out of water. He tried to blink the dust from his eyes as the corridor spun.

He reached blindly toward a muffled groan barely heard over the ringing. Armoured fingers fumbled absently around the rubble, but found no one.

"Father—" Amaury coughed as more bricks settled atop him.

He worked his shoulder free, leaving the shield trapped under the bricks.

Stumbling to his feet, Amaury could see the mountain of bricks and beams that had been pulled down upon them.

A laboured cry grabbed his attention.

Amaury stumbled on a loose brick as he turned to face the priest trapped beneath a thick wooden beam.

"Hold on, Father," Amaury gasped, steadying himself against the intact inner wall.

He wrapped his arms around the thick beam and pulled with every muscle of his body, but it wouldn't move.

Amaury exhaled, wiped the sweat from his brow and tried again.

"My son," the priest breathed, "my son." His weak hand touched Amaury's shoulder.

He struggled, ignoring the words as his face turned red. His breathing laboured as he released the unmoving beam finally and sat back on his heels to look at the priest.

"I can't leave you, Father."

"You must," Father Hugues gasped as blood coloured his lips, "take our Lord's cross." With a weak hand, the priest took his and pressed an egg-shaped staurotheke into his leathered palm. "See it to safety. May God bless and protect you, my son." Father Hugues made a slow sign of the cross over him.

Amaury tucked the reliquary beneath his surcoat so it rested over his heart. When he looked back, the priest had fallen still, empty eyes gazing towards the heavens.

"Requiescat in pace, Padre," Amaury said and closed the man's eyelids.

He turned back, gazing upon the rubble that had swallowed Sir Gérard by the catacomb entrance.

"Requiescat in pace, Sir Gérard," he said, crossing himself once more.

Shouts echoed outside the opening, followed by armoured shadows.

An arrow buried itself in the wooden beam.

Amaury rushed toward the opening where the gate had stood moments before the impact.

A second arrow ricocheted off the pile of bricks. Another soared past his ear, while others landed in the stone wall.

"Gah!" Amaury gasped as one struck his shoulder, burying itself past his chain-mail into his flesh.

His feet faltered.

Amaury tumbled down the steps, the arrow snapping as he hit the floor.

"Oh, my Lord—" Amaury gasped, his shoulder throbbing as he lay on the stone floor, "— have mercy on me, a sinner," he breathed and climbed to his feet.

Numbness had spread through his arm, and moving it caused hot pain to explode through his right side.

With his offhand, Amaury lifted a flickering torch from the wall and pushed forward, seeing the symbol Sir Gérard had shown him.

"You who dwell in the shelter of the Most High ..." Amaury recalled the comforting words of Psalm ninety-one as he dragged his beaten body through the tunnels.

Turning a corner, he hesitated at an arched threshold leading to an open chamber. It might have been a tomb, but the torch's weak light failed to reach far enough in for him to tell.

Amaury passed a quick glance around for any symbols to lead him on.

His eyes landed on an unusual marking inside the arch.

Brushing away a layer of lingering dust, Amaury could make out a circle with unfamiliar characters within. Whatever it was, he knew it wasn't a cross of Jerusalem.

He braced himself against the wall, breath uneven, blood dripping from his fingers as his armour seemed to drag him downward.

"Because he clings to me I will deliver him," Amaury exhaled, thinking to the relic held in place over his heart, "because he knows my name I will set him on high."

He took a deep inhale and pushed away from the wall.

With nowhere else to go, he continued onward, praying the lone path would lead him out.

The torch sputtered.

A gold shimmer seemed to fill the threshold. Amaury blinked, but the shimmer remained.

Thinking only of his duty, Amaury pressed on.

The gold streaks seemed to follow him, and the darkness grew thicker. Each step felt smaller, heavier, as though the passage itself were narrowing.

"He will call upon me, and I will answer," Amaury whispered, watching the torch dim until it was almost out.

Then, he saw the faint light glowing in the distance, growing brighter with each step forward.

The floor seemed to change from rough ground to smooth polished tile, and cool fresh air brushed against his cheekbones.

Amaury looked back toward the tunnel he'd come from, finding only a smooth grey wall. The archway was still intact, but noticeably more cracked and worn.

"I will be with him in distress..." Amaury whispered in disbelief as he touched the smooth, seamless wall, leaving a bloody mark behind.

He turned back to the strange open space around him.

Along the blindingly white wall, sat glass boxes containing various objects. Above the boxes was a dark sign with strange Latin text in gold and white:

Where Crusaders Walk

Crusader Europe and the Holy Land

He dragged himself toward the three armour sets on stands. A Knight Hospitaler and a Knight of the Temple stood side by side, but it was the third he gravitated toward.

He stood before the familiar set of armour, with its pristine red Cross of Jerusalem, but something seemed off about it. It seemed too clean, and the helmet too perfect.

"Oi!" a man shouted.

Amaury thought to reach for his sword, but the numbness had fully taken over and it refused to move. He moved to look at the man approaching from his left, but froze as a jolt of pain shot down his back.

"Mate, you can't have open flames." The man grabbed the dying torch before tossing it to the ground and throwing his dark coat atop the flame. "Are you with the Crusades exhibit? Where'd you even get that thing?"

"Que est ceste place? Est-ce Purgatorie?" Amaury asked in his native French as he struggled to turn and face the man.

"What? Purgatory? I don't know what you're on about, mate. This is ..." the man's words trailed off as he finally took a proper look at the battered knight before him, "... the British Museum. Do you need some help?"

Amaury stared at the man, unable to make out the language he spoke.

"Uh... Martin," the man said into a black box attached to his shoulder, "I've got one of your guys here, and he's bleeding pretty bad ... Looks like he got hit by a car or somethin."

Dryness burned in his chest as Amaury coughed and struggled against the exhaustion coming over him.

"What do you mean 'one of my guys'? There's no re-enactors scheduled for today," Another male voice crackled from the box.

Amaury's eyes grew wide, and he looked around for the ambient voice, his heart leaping in his chest.

Black spots dotted his vision.

He swallowed hard against his dry throat and stumbled backwards, dropping to one knee.

"Oh, shit — I need an ambulance for this guy."

Each breath became harder to take until finally he collapsed into the looming darkness.

"He must have come from Jerusalem — or Acre," Sophia stated as the footage of the crusader materializing through the wall of the museum exhibit repeated.

"What? From the 13th century?" Martin scowled, looking down at his watch. "This is the real world, Sophia. That's not possible."

"Fine," she said, dropping to the couch against the wall. "You tell me where else a period-accurate Knight of the Holy Sepulchre came from."

"I don't know," Martin sighed, rubbing his eyes. He must have watched the security video a hundred times now.

"I need to get to the hospital. Whoever the guy is, he's my responsibility until we figure out where he came from," he pushed back from the desk with a sigh and rose from his chair. This wasn't exactly how he'd planned to spend his evening.

"If we're lucky, he's awake and can answer some questions."

"I'm coming with you," Sophia said, jumping to her feet and grabbing her coat. "How else are you supposed to understand that old French he was speaking?"

"I could use Google Translate," Martin said, grabbing his own coat from the stand and headed for the door.

"Good luck with that," Sophia scoffed and closed the door of the office behind her.

"Right now, he's intubated and he'll be sedated until tomorrow. The surgery went well, though," the young woman wearing scrubs said, escorting them through the ICU.

"The surgery?" Martin asked.

"Yes. There was a foreign body removed from his shoulder. Heard it was an arrow," the nurse said raising her eyebrows as she stopped outside the door. "Let us know if you need anything." Then she walked away, probably to take care of something else on the unit.

They entered the room, settling into the visitor chairs on either side of the bed.

Martin looked over the battered man connected to the beeping heart monitor and wheezing ventilator. No questions tonight, he sighed to himself.

"So ... they would have cut his tunic and everything off..." Sophia said, looking across the bed at Martin.

"Yeah," rubbing his eyes, "at least he's not dead, I guess."

"Not yet."

"Sophia," he hissed and scowled at her, "don't say that!"

"What?! It's not like he could understand. Even if he was awake." She hissed back and crossed her arms. "We should have brought some flowers." She sat back in the chair, looking around the sterile hospital room.

"The gift shop is still open I think. If you want to grab some. Here." Martin stood, pulling his wallet from the pocket of his trousers and tossing ten pounds to Sophia. "I'm going to ask the nurses where his stuff got to."

"Trying to get rid of your wingman?" Sophia shot her head and plucked the note off the end of the bed.

"How else am I supposed to chat up the nurses?" Martin said with a chuckle as he headed from the quiet room.

The ICU was busy enough that evening, with alarms going off and nurses rushing between patients. The nurses station was decoration with different coloured paper eggs for the recently passed holiday.

"Excuse me," Martin said, leaning against the counter of the nursing station.

The older nurse looked up at him over her glasses as she continued to type on the computer.

"What do you need?"

"The man in room I14.1, do you know where his clothing and possessions have gotten off to?"

Her lips pursed, and she paused typing.

"Hmm... I think they've been handed over to the police, but I'll double-check if you can hold on a few minutes."

"Of course, thanks for checking," Martin said, heading back to the knight's room. He wasn't interested in towering over the woman while she worked.

He dropped back into the chair, lacing his fingers together as he relaxed as best as he could into the less-than-comfortable hospital chair. Martin was convinced they bought all these chairs without stuffing to save on costs.

"No promises mate, but I'll try to see they don't toss your stuff in the bin," he said to the unconscious man. If he had somehow come from the Crusades, Martin would be gutted to lose his tunic and everything he had been wearing. And the man also, obviously, Martin thought to himself as a flood of questions he wanted to ask jumped to mind.

"You asked about I14s things?" The older nurse asked.

Martin's heart leapt, and he looked toward the doorframe.

"Yes, I did." He sighed.

"Yeah, A&E handed his stuff over to the police already. You'll have to talk to them if you want to know anything else," she said around the doorframe.

"I will, thank you."

She nodded a welcome as she headed away.

"Well… at least they're somewhere other than the bin," Martin said with a shrug.

"You know, these will probably be the nicest flowers this guy's ever seen." Sophia spoke, half to herself, as she stepped back into the room and placed the flowers on the bedside table next to the man.

"So, it sounds like his stuff is with the police. I'll have to call the station tomorrow; they wanted a copy of the CCTV footage anyway."

"Do you want to get going then?" Sophia asked, looking away from the vase of flowers.

"Yeah, let's head off." Martin rose to his feet, pulling his coat back on.

"Let's grab a take-away. I'll buy." Sophia pulled on her own coat and headed from the room.

"It's your turn anyway." Martin chuckled half-heartedly and followed her from the room.

The lights of the ward dimmed as they headed away, leaving the displaced knight to rest with the sound of the beeping heart monitor next to him.

FIN

The Multi-Verses Theory

Greg Shedden

Lacey felt her blood pressure rise when Bill Langston trashed the show they had just watched.

"Alien abductions, Bigfoot, time travellers with iPhones in pictures from the late 1800s, it's all BS I tell you," Bill argued. He cleared the dishes from the coffee table of the small bachelor-style apartment he and Lacey shared. "I will give you, there could be and likely is, life out there in the vast universe but any alien life forms that have the technology to travel through space from some planet light-years away would not, upon arrival, decide that an anal probe of some hillbilly from the Ozarks would be the best use of their time."

Lacey enjoyed reading about mysterious sightings and UFOs and had even picked up a National Enquirer on occasion. *Bill is more closed-minded than he's willing to accept*, she thought as she loaded the dishwasher, determined to justify her thinking to Bill. "All I am saying is that there are more things we don't know than there are things we do," she said. There was a guy, his name was Everett something. He was a ... like a really important scientist in, like the fifties or sixties, and he argued there could be many planes of reality or like different universes all existing at the same time. And this guy, Neil Tyson, I think his name is; he even has a video out explaining how this could be, like real."

"What the hell has that got to do with alien abductions or time travelling kids holding iPhones?" Bill said reaching into the cupboard under the kitchen sink to toss some paper napkins into a small trash can.

"C'mon, think," Lacey replied, "These guys say it's possible that these different universes could accidentally cross over one another or link up or something, and if that happened then some weird crap could go down. So, like maybe if there is a life form in another universe and it found itself suddenly looking down at a planet that wasn't even supposed to exist, well then, they would want to check that place out, right?"

"So, maybe the, you know, the anal probe thing is stupid but maybe not," she continued. "I bet scientists who study insects, like maybe they might want to do an anal probe on a living insect to test the poop. I read that scientists can learn a lot from studying an animal's poop." She sat down on their ancient, overstuffed, flower-print sofa and cocked her head as a show of having scored a point.

"So, they start to study this creature they have captured and then decide, heck, maybe we should put this creature back where we found it," Bill said with an exaggerated eye roll. He sat on the arm of the sofa. "And then what, they just decide to move on?"

Lacey gave Bill's knees a little push, crossed her arms and answered, "Ok look, I don't pretend to have all the answers, but what I don't do is just totally shut down the idea that something like that could happen. Maybe, they decide they would like to watch 'the creature' interact with its normal environment but before they get to further their study, wham, the connection between the two universes breaks and they are sitting in their spaceship thinking, holy shit, did any of that really happen?"

Bill laughed. "And, Bigfoot and the Loch Ness monster, are they creatures from one of these crossover universes?"

"Maybe," Lacey answered. "Maybe there are other explanations. What I like to do, and I would argue, all thinking people should do, is to have an open mind and consider the possibilities instead of just labelling people as nut-jobs because they believe they saw something that they cannot explain."

"Crap, it's already after midnight," he interrupted glancing at the digital display on the oven's clock. "We were supposed to be meeting everybody at the bar after the concert was over. They have to be there by now."

"Let's go then," Lacey suggested, getting up and grabbing her jacket from the back of one of the kitchen chairs. "If they aren't there yet they will be soon."

The sports bar that Lacey and her friends frequented was loud and lively when she and Bill arrived. A hint of marijuana smoke greeted them as they paid a burly bouncer the cover fee and made their way into the mayhem. The Jayhawks, the local college football team, had just secured a playoff spot, and the red-hot Cougars, the local triple-A baseball team, had also won that night. Fans of both teams were celebrating. Add the crowd from the Electric Thunder concert that had just let out and, well, you had chaos. The deep bass beat of whatever techno music the D.J. was playing was barely discernible over the rest of the noise.

Lacey waited for her eyes to adjust to the dim lighting and then craned her neck to scan the room. "I see them over in the corner!" she yelled. "Go get us a couple of beers and I'll see if I can find us some seats."

"Ok, but you're going to have to pay me back!' Bill yelled. "I ain't made of money!"

Bill's best friend Jay Reynolds was huddled in the back corner at a small table with his cousin Terry Alexander. Beneath the low hanging neon Coors beer sign Richard Meyer's head glowed red across from them.

"I still think that Rose-Coloured Kaleidoscopes is their best song," Terry said, as Lacey came within earshot of what was obviously a very intense conversation.

"It's just a little too weird for me," Jay replied. "Clearly 'Our Dying Planet' was their biggest hit and it's my favourite."

"Hey guys!" Lacey called out, putting an arm around Terry's shoulders. "Rich, can you see if there are extra chairs anywhere? Bill is getting our drinks."

"Hey," answered each of her friends in chorus.

"Wish me luck," Richard joked setting out into the melee.

Terry stood to give Lacey a sideways hug. "How was the movie?" he said.

"We didn't end up going." Lacey said. "I had to apologize to Bill but I've heard that that British guy Anthony Hopkins is, like, really psycho scary in the movie and, well I just ... Bill was good about it. We ended up watching that T.V. show, Unexplained Mysteries."

Richard brought over two rather flimsy-looking black folding chairs. Lacey thanked him with a nod and a wink and then chose the sturdiest of the two as her seat.

"And then," Bill interjected handing Lacey her beer, "we got into a big discussion about aliens and Bigfoot and other weird-ass stuff." Bill looked at the empty chair that Richard had put out for him. "Thanks anyway, Rich, but that thing really doesn't look stable to me. I'll just stand."

"Bill thinks I am too into all that Unexplained Mysteries stuff," Lacey said with a laugh.She took a long pull on her beer. "Umm, where is Allan, I thought he was supposed to have gone to the concert with you?"

"Oh, he's here somewhere," Jay answered with a chuckle. "He saw Shawna when we came in and decided to take his best shot now that she is single again."

"Shawna Williams?" Bill said, leaning back against the rough brick wall while being careful not to knock the Coors sign. "Wasn't' she seeing Ted Rogers?"

"Yeah, but they broke up, again," Terry replied with a shrug of his shoulders. "Allan has had a crush on her for like, ever, and he's had a few shots of liquid courage, so..."

The conversation moved from the multi-universe theory back to the music of Electric Thunder and then for half an hour they consoled Allan, who had struck out with 'the beautiful and amazing Shawna Williams'.

By 2:30 am everyone was well lubricated and growing tired. The energy of the bar was waning; the D.J. had ended his last set and the heavy smells of sweat, spilled beer, and the lingering odour of the joints smoked in the bathrooms served as signals to call it a night. Jay and Terry were the first to head back to their apartment, a rather shabby little place over Ling's Chinese Restaurant.

Allan mentioned he had a six-pack of Millers back at his place, a two-bedroom little clapboard house he shared with three other guys. He convinced Lacey, Bill and Richard that, as long as they were quiet, they could polish off the beers in the basement den without causing problems with his roomies.

"I'm telling you, Jay," Lacey insisted. "We have had this exact conversation."

"And I'm telling you, Lacey, we haven't," answered her confused boyfriend, Jay. "Like I would forget an argument about Bigfoot and time travel and, let's not forget, imaginary multi-verses."

"Wow, ok," Lacey mumbled while getting up to grab her jacket from the back of a kitchen chair. It was time to leave for their walk to Cuppa Joe, a local cafe frequented by Jay, Lacey and their friends. "I think we had better add déjà vu to that list of unexplained phenomena, cuz I have just had the longest version of that ever."

"I think I read something about brain processes that is supposed to explain déjà vu," Jay suggested, grabbing his own coat and wallet. He followed Lacey to the door of their small, rent-controlled apartment.

They made their way to the cafe, and Lacey could not shake the feeling that she and Jay really had a long conversation about the multi-verses theory before. She was a bit weirded out by the fact that Jay was just as certain that they had not.

The usual gang of Lacey and Jay's friends were at the cafe when they arrived and took in the familiar and much appreciated smell of freshly brewed coffee. Bill, Jay's best friend, Terry, Bill's long-time boyfriend and Richard huddled around a small round table in a back corner of the cafe staring at a Monopoly board. Lacey and Jay gave their friends a wave after shaking off the evening's rain from their jackets. Karen, one of two teen girls who worked the evening shifts, called out to Jay asking if he and Lacey were having their usual, a large cafe mocha for him and an Americano black with a splash of cream for Lacey, and received a thumbs up from Jay.

"Hey guys!" Lacey called out, throwing an arm around Terry's shoulders. "Rich, can you help me find a couple of chairs? Jay is getting our drinks."

"Hey," answered each of her friends in chorus.

"How was the play?" Terry said, standing to give Lacey a sideways hug.

Richard brought over two high-backed wooden chairs. Lacey thanked him with a nod and a wink and then turned to answer Terry's question.

"We didn't end up going," Lacey said. "I had to apologize to Jay, but I've heard that the play we were going to see, called Angels in

America, is a bit edgy and well, I just wanted to stay home and relax, so we watched T.V. instead."

"And then," Jay added, handing Lacey her coffee and taking a seat beside her. "We got into a big discussion about aliens and Bigfoot and other weird-ass stuff."

"Yeah, Jay thinks I am like, too into all that Unexplained Mysteries stuff," Lacey laughed before blowing across the top of her hot drink. "Umm, where is Allan, I thought he was supposed to be joining us?"

"Oh, he's here somewhere," Bill answered with a chuckle. "He saw Shawna Williams when we came in and decided to take his best shot now that she is single again."

The conversation moved from the topic of multi-verses back to the Monopoly board game, and then for half an hour they consoled Allan, who had struck out with 'the beautiful and amazing Shawna Willams'.

By 11:13 pm interest in the game was waning and the small group of friends were the only customers left in the shop. Karen put covers over the now emptied and cleaned coffee machines and was busy cashing out her till. Bill and Terry were the first to announce their decision to head back to their apartment. They lived in a rather shabby little place over Ling's Chinese Restaurant which was located only a couple of blocks away from the cafe on Elmwood Street.

Allan mentioned he had a six-pack of Millers at his place, a two-bedroom little clapboard house he shared with three other guys. He convinced Jay and Richard Meyers that, as long as they were quiet, they could polish off the beers in the basement den without causing problems with his roomies. Lacey thanked Allan for the invitation, told Jay that she was tired and promised she would text him when she got home. She was determined to do some Googling about déjà vu experiences in the hopes she could find some peace of mind. Their argument was still really upsetting her.

"I'm telling you, Terry," Lacey insisted, "we have had this exact conversation."

"And I'm telling you, Lacey, we haven't," answered her confused boyfriend, Terry. "Like I would forget an argument about Bigfoot and time travel and, let's not forget, an imaginary multi-verse."

"Wow, ok," Lacey mumbled while getting up and grabbing her backpack and jacket for their walk to the fitness centre. "I ... I just don't understand why it felt so... really odd. I guess maybe I had a dream like this."

Terry grabbed his gym bag, wallet, and keys, and then followed Lacey out the door, double-checking to ensure that the apartment door was locked.

Terry linked arms with Lacey and asked, "You okay? This dream thing seems to have you a little spooked."

"Yeah, sorry," Lacey answered, "but yeah, I am a little freaked about how certain I was that we had talked about the multi-verses thing." Except it was more than that. Lacey's thoughts were bouncing from one possibility to another. Terry was probably right; he would almost certainly have remembered a conversation about aliens crossing over from one universal plane to another, but Lacey was equally certain they'd had that discussion.

The usual gang of Lacey and Terry's friends were already at the treadmills when they arrived at Gerry's Gym and Spa, which was a spacious, well-lit, modern facility that the owners kept immaculately clean. Bill and his best friend Terry were running hard while Bill's sister Jay was maintaining an easy jog. Richard Meyers was doing bench presses at the nearby weight station. Lacey decided she would not let her troubled thoughts ruin her workout. She laced her runners and headed over to her friends, who were all gathered at a set of treadmills.

"Hey guys!" she called out. "Yo, Rich, looking good. What weight are you up to?"

"Hey," answered each of her friends in chorus.

Richard let out a deep grunt and replaced his weights on the stand. "I am benching 180," he answered.

"How's it going?" Jay said, hopping off his treadmill to give Lacey a sideways hug and gesturing that the machine was hers for the taking.

Lacey gave Richard an enthusiastic two thumbs up and then set her favourite routine on the control panel of the open treadmill.

"Hey, did you guys enjoy that matinee you were planning to see?" Richard said.

"We didn't end up going," Lacey answered, beginning a slow jog. "I had to apologize to Terry, but I've heard that the play, Angels in America, is edgy and well, I just wanted to stay home and relax, so we watched T.V. instead. I YouTubed an episode of Unexplained Mysteries I wanted to watch."

"And then," Terry interjected, placing Lacey's water bottle in the treadmill's cup holder, "we got into a big discussion about aliens and Bigfoot and other weird-ass stuff."

"Yeah, Terry thinks I am, like, too into all that Unexplained Mysteries stuff," Lacey laughed a little nervously. She took a swig from the water bottle and then increased the pace of her run. "And, while we were talking, I had the most bizarre déjà vu experience, or maybe I was remembering a very vivid dream. Thing was, I felt sure we had had the whole conversation before."

But wait, Lacey thought, stumbling for a second on her machine. *It wasn't Terry I was talking to about the multi-verse idea. In my dream, or whatever it was, I was arguing with Bill or, shit, maybe it was Jay.*

Terry stepped off his machine and walked over to her and whispered, "Hey really, are you alright?"

Lacey looked into Terry's eyes and, noticing his concern, decided they would have to talk about things later. It was too heavy a conversation to have at that moment. She gave him a quick kiss. "Yeah, I guess I am just a little tired."

Allan showed up quite disconsolate at having been rejected by 'the amazing Shawna Williams, a girl he had long had a crush on, but who had been dating a local sports hero named Ted Rogers.

Everyone finished their workouts and then they joined up at the smoothie bar and spent a half an hour consoling Allan.

At 9:30 pm Bill and Jay announced their decision to head home. They still lived with their parents, and it was a bit of a drive back to the burbs. Allan mentioned he had a six-pack of Millers at his place, a two-bedroom little clapboard house he shared with three other guys. He convinced Terry and Richard to help him polish off the beers in the basement den before they called it a night.

Lacey promised Terry that she would be fine, that she would text him when she got home and would probably feel better after a good night's sleep. Terry promised he would not be too late, and he would be sure to be quiet when he came to bed.

Lacey struggled to pull up the zipper on her jacket as she left the gym and began her walk home in the cold night air. She was caught up in her jumbled thoughts and nearly walked out in front of an oncoming car. Upon arrival at her apartment, she took a sleeping pill and prayed that everything would make more sense in the morning.

"We were watching an episode of this old show, Unexplained Mysteries," Allan said to the two police officers that had answered his 911 call. "I told her, I just don't buy any of this shit and she just started laughing weirdly and then cried hysterically. She keeps saying that she can't keep jumping around. I have no idea what she is talking about."

"It's not right... I ... I can't keep doing this over and over and over..." Lacey whispered to the EMT that was trying to give her a shot to calm her down.

The End

Final Draft

Scarlett Kol

"So James, are Paradox and Lord Anarchy ever gonna do it?" He bellows the loud question over the audience and ends his comment with a piggish snort, although no one else is laughing.

I sigh and stare at my water glass. Here we go again–the sex question. It comes up at least once per panel, but still brings on a warm acid-tasting substance in my mouth. The kinky stuff is for the romance girls in the auditorium down the hall. My books are action adventures, not some sticky-paged filth that you leave on the toilet tank. Paradox Steel deserves better. She isn't a disposable fix. Why didn't people get that?

The pimply-faced guy stands waiting for an answer. The slick from too much hair gel and not enough exercise visible from the stage.

Conjuring my least annoyed tone and even managing a weak thin-lipped smile, I reply, "I guess you'll have to wait for book seven."

Crater Face nods and sits down as the crowd erupts in applause.

It's not a satisfying response, but at least my agent will be happy I am plugging my upcoming release. She insists that I work on my 'platform' and improve my 'marketability'. Whatever happened to writers who just write?

The side door clicks open. A kid in a convention t-shirt gives the silent open hand five-minute warning.

Finally.

"Any closing comments?" the moderator asks. A room of intent eyes stares up at me waiting for wisdom.

I rub my forehead, trying to look like I'm pulling wisdom from some deep dark place. "Write about what you love. At least one person will like your stuff."

A few chuckles. My shoulders drop. It's meant to be funny but sometimes falls flat.

People shuffle out. I hang back. If you get too close they ask more questions.

I close my eyes. Last panel of the day. A few hours of signing tomorrow and I will be on a plane home. Maybe I can lock myself in my loft for a few days. Order a week's worth of Chinese from Double Rainbow and shut all the blinds. A real world detox. That would be awesome.

"Hey Starks."

I look up. It's Chris Kutati from the Mystic Warrior series. We've been on the same panel circuit for the past couple years. Seems like a good guy. Or at least he hasn't done anything to trip my jerk meter yet.

"A few of us are going to hit the lobby bar. Interested?" Tempting. A whiskey and soda might erase at least some of this day. A warm feeling rushes through my chest as I almost taste the burn on my tongue. "No sorry. Got a huge list of edits to get through."

"Work, work, work Starks." He thumps me on the back and I lurch forward. "You'll make us all look bad. But I guess that's why you outsell me every time."

I shrug. "Sorry."

He backs toward the door. "If you change your mind ..." He mimes double finger guns at me and disappears into the hall.

I scan the empty chairs of the auditorium and revel in the silence. One day down, only one more to go.

The room service steak is tough but decent, except the beer is warm as midday sun. A few cold ones at the bar would be great about now, but better not. Far too much work to do.

I lied to Chris about the list of edits. In truth, only one edit remains, but it's plaguing me. I have no idea how I'm going to end this book. Paradox Steel has already taken down evil super villain Lacerax in an incredible action sequence that involved chopping off his saw hand and blowing up half of the city, but it wasn't enough. Just a half-assed scene that pleased enough people to get this far in the editing process, but still doesn't feel right. It needs more. Something stronger. A hook. One final thrust for the reader to hang onto until they can preorder book eight. It feels unfinished. Broken.

The cursor blinks at me. I stare at it, hoping to be inspired. Maybe I should just write some smut and get people off my back. But no. It's not me. It isn't her either.

I settle on something reflective with a bit of a twist, but it still doesn't satisfy. I highlight the entire thing and hit delete. What is it now, the twentieth time I've started over?

I shut the laptop, slide it into its bag, and pull out the cover mock-up.

It's a good cover. A glossy deep purple with plenty of ominous shadows and a noir looking cityscape. The classic red 'J. Starkling' in Comic Book Bold Italic and the one-word title 'Bittersweet' across the top. My editor hated the title. Too feminine, he said. But like the other books, the title needed to be paradoxical and sales of the prior installment rang high enough to allow some creative license. Besides Para always picked her own titles. Fifteen years of living in my screwed-up brain warranted naming rights.

In the center of the cover stands Paradox. She faces the city but then twists at the hip, looking back toward the reader. Her hands crisscross behind her clutching her signature twin sai. Her green and silver suit pulls tight against her body, accentuating every voluptuous curve. Marketing modified her since the last book—again. Her boobs are bigger, her waist smaller. If she stepped off the page like that, she probably wouldn't be able to stand, let alone walk. Why couldn't they leave her alone? The real her is already perfect. Just as I'd written her. At least I think so.

I look around. My view is hazy at the edges as I take in the ugly hotel curtains and the generic stock photo art on the walls. I rub my hands over my face. I'm not going to get anywhere on this tonight.

Lying down isn't much better. The itchy sheets tell my skin that I'm not in my own bed.

Worst of all, I can't get my brain to shut off. I pull the pillow over my head. The sanitary scent of bleach burns in my nostrils as my eyes begin to close.

It's cold. Dark. A pungent dirty smell taints the clean one I remember. Urine mixed with rotting garbage. Brick walls tower on either side and inks shadows on the ground. A blur of headlights stream by at the end of the alley. I shake my head and steady myself against the wall. Where am I? A siren wails past. The click of heels thunder on the pavement, echoing closer.

"Para?"

She appears out of the darkness. The filtered moonlight cuts stripes across her face.

"James." She grabs my hand. Her soft skin slips against my calloused fingers. Flesh so much better than the memory. "There's not much time."

"What's going on? Where are we?"

I scan the looming midnight. Not another soul. Just us in this rank alleyway. An unlikely meeting spot. Dangerous. Couldn't we go back to her place?

"Something's coming," her alluring whisper edges with trepidation. She shivers.

I pull her close with my free arm, as my other hand crushes into her chest. My chin rests in her hair. Vanilla and raspberries. "Whatever it is, we'll get through it."

She pushes away and stares up at me, dark eyes wide. "It's not me. Something's coming for you. I don't know if I can stop it."

She rises on tiptoe and presses her cinnamon red lips to mine. There's urgency. Not like all the other times. I try to hold onto her, but she slides away.

"I love you, James."

Her leather trench coat flaps behind her. She pauses near the street and glances back. One last time. Her lips pout as an ominous fear slides through her eyes. She blinks. Then she's gone.

I awaken. The alarm buzzes with an irritating drone. Did it actually wake me or did I come to on my own? I silence it with a smack and roll back over. I still smell her on my skin. Vanilla and raspberries. I inhale deeper.

The convention center is already thrumming. My head throbs. Shouldn't have lost count of last night's beer. I elbow my way through the growing horde as they zig and zag between the endless rows of booths like children high on Pixy Stixs and slushies. Overhead, a drone zooms around nearly clipping the top of the acid green volunteer tent. I grab ahold of a nearby table to keep the room from spinning as the whole event suddenly feels like a fever dream and I can't wake up. A pile of manga comics splash across the floor. I mouth a curt apology and move to pick them up, but the proprietor drops their furry cartoon fox head my direction as if to tell me to bugger off.

Trust me, buddy, I don't want to be here either.

Finally, I reach the far back corner of the hall. Artist's Alley they affectionately call it, but it's just a way to corral us away from the bustling lines of the real celebrities or the merchants trying to make an actual profit at these things. But even after all these years, I can still draw a decent crowd, or at least my publisher can.

Life size cardboard cutouts of my characters flank my booth. Arranged with precision like chess pieces. A covered table sits prominent in the middle, piled high with books. A large "World of Paradox Steel" banner above the display waves in the flow of the air conditioner. Today is going to be a long day.

I take my seat as a small line starts to form. I sigh. Para's words echo in my pounding brain. Something's coming. But what?

I examine the fans. Excited smiles and glassy eyes. Nothing to fear, but it still feels off. A heaviness weighs on my neck and shoulders. Am I being watched? Of course, I am. Everyone within twenty feet wants a part of this world. This is what they came to see. I'm their dancing writer monkey. Except, this doesn't feel the same. I've been to a ton of these things before. Why is it different now?

I ache to see Para again, but it'll have to wait. I need to focus. At least for a few hours. I shake my head and push out my memories of last night. All but that kiss, allowing the sweet taste of her to linger on my lips and get me through this day.

The flood begins. Book after book in varying states of care smack down in front of me. I sign and smile. Smile and sign.

I get a lot of guys at my booth. No surprise. Most are quiet and shy. They ask questions about where I get my ideas and provide their theories on the future of the series. I tell them what they want to hear—training courtesy of my agent—and they go on their way.

Most girls dress as Paradox. Actually, *like* Paradox, as not one ever gets it right. Too skinny. Too chunky. Too blonde. And Para would never wear that hideous bubble gum pink lipstick. They lack her elegance. But it's not their fault. They don't know her like I do. No one does. The heaviness on my back drags harder.

A stack of well-worn books slams down on the table in front of me. I look up. Crater Face from yesterday. A lecherous smile curls across his lips.

I shudder. "Who do I make it out to?" *Billy Joe Scumbag?*

"Steve."

I don't bother asking a last name. I want him gone.

Steve scoops up his books and gives the cardboard Paradox a once over before slinking away. I cringe.

The feeling is back. I look around again. This time someone is staring. He vanishes for a moment between the swaths of fans outfitted as wizards, orcs, and anime something or others, then reappears in the same spot, still staring, as if only the two of us exist.

A man. A tall man. Dressed in black. All black. His baseball hat to his combat boots. He stares at me from across the room. Convention goers putter around him, but he stands motionless, staring, boring into my head. Could this be the something Para had warned me about? No. Just another creep.

"There's only one 'L' in Ashley." A red-headed imitation Paradox crosses her arms and begins to pout.

My face heats up. I grab a display copy of book five 'Beginning of the End' and thrust it into her hands. "Take this. Enjoy the Con."

I look again, but the man in black is gone.

Deep breath.

The morning plods along. My ears ring as the constant hum of voices mixes with the pounding electronic thump from the overhead speakers.

"Who can I make this out to?" I ask for the millionth time, as my brain aches in my skull.

A rusted saw blade drops onto the table. No book copy. I tense and look up. The man in black looms over my table.

He smiles at me. A line of teeth glowing white against his suntanned unshaven face. A chill slithers up my spine as I jerk my head back.

"I like the villains." His voice rasps. Menacing.

I swallow hard. My leg taps, shaking the table cloth. Sound falls away. Movements slowing to a near pause. Para's face flashes in my head. *Something's coming.* Then the man's toothy smile. My breath catches in my lungs. I glance down the long line still leading from my table and the faces slip in and out of focus, all the costumes melding into something straight from a nightmare.

The man leans across my table, too close, as the sharp tang of sweat prickles in my nostrils.

"I've been waiting a long time for this," he hisses.

My heartbeat skips. I clutch my chest and thrust my chair backwards.

I run.

Immediately, I slam into the Lord Anarchy cut out. I trip forward, the figure caught in my feet. I toss it behind me and take off into the gawking crowd.

Shrieks and grumbles lay in my wake as I push my way through to the side of the room to a clearer path.

I glance back. The man in black is giving chase his long jacket flapping like a cape behind him. Except he's no hero.

Bam! My shoulder slams right into a cosplaying robot. I falter but keep sprinting. It bleeps something unbecoming of a cyborg as I keep going.

My thoughts jumble in my brain. He came at me, right? Any rational person would see that. Wouldn't they? My agent is going to murder me. Confused faces blur past, but my feet won't stop running.

"Hey!" The booming voice of the man in black yells from behind me. "Where's my autograph?"

I ignore him and escape through the side exit door. Five flights of stairs, two at a time. I'm clearly not made for running as I wheeze and cough the rest of the way.

I click the deadbolt home and double over panting against the hotel room door. My brow is dripping and I rub my sweaty hands down my thighs.

What is wrong with me? I replay the scene in my muddled brain and the reality hits me like the hammer of a god. I ran like a coward through a packed convention to get away from a fan, albeit a weird one. For what? Because I can't get my head straight after Para's warning. I can't keep doing this.

Her world has consumed mine. Every thought, every action, every dream is of her. For her. I'm nothing without her anymore, but everyone else wants a piece of her too.

I can barely remember when it was just the two of us. No one picking her apart. No sickos needing to taint her. Us.

My breathing slows, and my thoughts begin to focus. I want things back the way they used to be. I want out.

I rip my laptop open and begin to type. Seven would be the last book in series. Lucky seven. I finally found my ending. Now to write the last thing anyone would remember of her and her world. It needed to be perfect. Paradox Steel had to die, and I would be the one to kill her.

My fingers fly over the laptop keys. The afternoon sun cutting from the side of the blinds fades into night. Beads of sweat trickle down my spine. This was it and it was brilliant. Thoughtful without being melodramatic. Unexpected without compromising her character. The world could go away now. No more publicity. Just me and her, together always.

I type 'the end' and collapse in the chair. A lightness flows through me. It's done.

I close my eyes as the euphoria gives way to panic. A strange feeling builds in my throat, like dry bread lodged in my esophagus. I try to swallow. It doesn't move. I grope at my neck as I begin to cough, gasping for breath. The bleak hotel room swirls in front of me. A kaleidoscope spinning of bright whites and muted browns spiraling in flashes before my eyes. What is happening to me?

My left arm falls limp at my side. Why am I so weak? My chest tightens.

Para's face appears. She smiles a consoling smile. I reach to touch her, but my fingers slide through her image. An invisible knife stabs through my ribcage. One. Two. Three times. Para blows me a kiss from her perfect lips and fades into the abyss.

I glance at the last words on the screen. Two words. Six letters. My inevitable truth. The knife stabs again. My heart explodes.

Goodbye my love.

Darkness.

The End

Oathbound

Tania Stephanson

Gold font gleams over the azure-blue hardcover, with an image of a sword wrapped in vines and blooms of red roses. My favourite book. One that is filled with magic, lust for power, romance, and war. The heroine reminds me of my older sister, strong and beautiful, unwilling to bend to anyone else's will. Nothing like me, quiet and reserved, always dreaming of other worlds that only exist in fiction. I run my fingers over the title, Oathbound, which is raised just enough to feel the word against my skin. It sucks that I must replace my copy, which was all but destroyed in the basement flood.

Inhaling the enticing scent of a new book, I pull Oathbound tight against my chest, hugging it close to my heart, and continue through the aisles of the bookstore. The only thing I cannot replace is the author's signature on the title page, with a personalized note. *Ava, dream big and you will go far,* it had said. The dream of that book never being ruined in the first place is one that will never come true.

So many new books to choose from, and I can't afford to buy more than a few. The sale section had nothing of interest, which was disappointing. Maybe I can buy one each pay and slowly rebuild my home library. Movement catches my gaze in the far corner next to a bookshelf. On the floor is a shadow, small and unusual, the owner having large feral ears and hair sticking out all over. A creature of some sort that doesn't belong in the store, never mind this world. It's probably a child wearing a silly hat and a fluffy sweater. Laughter bubbles up, and I cover my mouth. Nothing worse than snort-laughing in public.

Curiosity overtakes me, and I move two rows ahead, then freeze in place. The figure peers around the corner of the shelf, staring at me with beady eyes. This is no child. It blinks once, then scurries in plain view to the corner of the store and enters a storage room. The way its scraggly body almost skipped across the room makes my stomach tight with laughter.

In disbelief, I rush toward the doorway and follow it inside. Stacks of boxes line the walls; each covered in labels belonging to various book suppliers or printing companies. The creature holds something in its slender fingers, long claws tapping on it. He glares at me, as if it's my fault that I saw him.

"Hey there," I say, hoping to calm its nerves. The thing gives me the creeps, but strangely he's kind of cute.

Its mouth opens, and he hisses like a cat before vanishing in a blinding flash of light. My heart-rate thunders in my ears and I rub my eyes with the back of my hand. I consider myself open-minded, but this is far beyond anything my imagination could have conjured up.

"What are you doing back here?" a male voice says behind me.

I turn to face a store employee wearing a blue vest and a sour expression. The boy must be in his late teens to early twenties, with brown, bushy hair and worn-out runners.

"Sorry," I say. "I was looking for the bathroom."

His expression relaxes, and he examines me. "Are you going to pay for that?"

My knuckles are white from gripping Oathbound so tight. "Of course, maybe you can hold it at the front counter for me while I find your bathroom?"

The boy smiles and holds out his hands. "The facilities are in the hallway near the till."

I hand him the book and walk past him to leave the storage room. In a daze, I wander through the store, and once inside the single-occupant restroom, I lock the door, my hands trembling. At the sink, I splash my face with cold water and dry off with paper towels. My skin is pale and eyes are wide as I stare at myself in the mirror. With the stress of the flood and dealing with the insurance company, I haven't slept properly. It's no wonder I'm seeing things. Maybe I need to get some sleep.

After paying for the replacement Oathbound novel, I head home and crawl into bed. Images of that creature flash through my mind, making it difficult to fall asleep. I turn on the touch-lamp next to the bed and grab the book lying next to it. It's been years since I've read this. Maybe it will alter my train of thoughts and help me fall asleep.

Page after page, I read Oathbound, recalling my favourite scenes and characters. One paragraph makes me stop. I read it three times, taking in every word. It describes a pesky creature that sneaks around at night, stealing precious objects, hoarding jewels and gemstones. The beast has ears larger than its head, sharp claws, and hair that sticks out as if an electric shock made it stand on end.

The creature in the library, the one that wasn't actually there; the description in the book matches what I saw precisely. Yet, I forgot about these guys from Oathbound until now. Is it possible my subconscious mind brought that image to the bizarre daydream? In my hands, the book feels warm. How long have I been reading? Yawning, I close the novel and set it on the nightstand, then touch the lamp, shutting it off.

Time passes during my restless sleep, my legs antsy, sliding back and forth. A clatter disturbs my failed attempt at peaceful slumber. I turn on the lamp, put on my slippers and use my cell phone's flashlight to wander down the hallway. Another clatter. It's coming from the kitchen. Reaching the entrance, I peek around the corner. Pots and pans sprawl across the floor. With the cupboard door open, it's impossible to see what's inside it.

On the counter is the wooden block holding steak knives; I grab one. Raccoons couldn't get inside, could they? I know I locked my door and there were no critters in sight. Step by step, I make my way to the rummager beneath the counter. I look over the top of the opened door, shining my light on the creature. The same one from the library.

"Hey," I say. "Stop that."

Wide, beady eyes glare at me. His ears barely fit inside the cupboard space. The thing grumbles and chatters at me incoherently.

My heart-rate pounds in my chest. This can't be happening. I must be asleep still.

A blinding light flashes from the living room, and the creature follows my gaze. He scrambles out of the cupboard, pulls an object out of the pouch that hangs from his belt, and vanishes.

Blinking, I stare at the spot he once stood.

A man clears his throat.

Stunned back to reality, I aim the phone's flashlight toward the living room to find a man in shining armour who stands with a sword at the ready.

"Who the fuck are you?" I say, backing away, holding the small steak knife in my left hand and my phone in the right. Up and down, I shine the flashlight on him, examining his giant metal boots and chest piece. "And what the hell are you doing in my house?"

"Where is he?" he says, his gaze darting around the kitchen.

"I'm the only one here," I reply.

"The aeggling." He lowers his weapon but keeps it in hand.

That's what they are called. I hadn't read far enough in the replacement book to find it. "Ah, yes, he disappeared." This is a strange-ass dream.

With a sigh, the knight sheathes his sword and removes his helmet. Thick blonde waves fall to his shoulders.

I shine my flashlight into his face, mouth gaping.

"Must you?" he says, shielding his piercing blue eyes. He is the mirror image of the perfect knight.

"Sorry." I lower the phone and reach over the counter to flick on the light.

A deep scar stretches across the left side of his face, reaching from beside his eye to just above his upper lip. Staring at me, a smile emerges on his perfect face. "Why, hello there," he says, leaning on the counter like a sly cat.

My cheeks flush. "Wait, I think I know who you are."

"Most do. I'm quite famous, you know." He winks.

"You're Shawn from... my book, Oathbound." My stomach flutters with excitement.

The gorgeous knight nods.

"And you are right here, in my kitchen."

He nods again, an air of arrogance expanding around him. "Yes, yes, I am." Shawn's expression becomes grim. "Where is he?" He leaves the kitchen and marches through the house.

"Where are you going?" I say, struggling to keep up with him. "I told you, he vanished."

Over his shoulder, Shawn shouts, "don't let him fool you, damsel! That little devil has not left the vicinity."

I choke on a laugh. "I'm not a damsel! You're in the real world, buddy. I'm just Ava."

Shawn pauses at my bedroom door and glances my way. "Alright, just Ava. Have no fear, Shawn of the Dreaded Mountains is here to save the day!"

He never talked like this in the book. What's wrong with him?

In my room, he lifts the edge of the large, pink floral quilt and searches under the bed. Next, he opens my closet door. Blouses and dresses drop to the floor, hangers still attached.

"Stop this!" I shout. "Get out of my room."

Shawn tosses item after item out of my closet: old books, childhood drawings and other memories I almost forgot existed. "Where are you, beast?" he shouts. Growling in frustration, he returns to the bed and stops at the nightstand.

"Don't even think about opening the top drawer; there's private girl stuff in there." I rush over and plant a protective hand against the drawer.

Shawn doesn't reply.

I follow his gaze to the book on my nightstand: Oathbound.

"You have the Sacred Text," he whispers. "How... how did this get into *your* possession?" Both of his hands hover over the emblem on the cover as if it offers warmth on a chilly day.

With a shrug, I answer, "I bought it."

Shawn meets my gaze. "That means..." He drops to his knees and pounds a fist over his chest, creating a loud bong sound. "You are the Oath Master."

That's it. I've lost my marbles. "Alright, where's the camera?" I search the room, every corner, lifting ornaments and moving furniture around.

"What is it, Master?" Shawn asks as he shadows my every move.

Hands on my hips, I glare at him. "This is quite the prank, *Shawn*. Or whatever your real name is."

"A prank? 'Tis nothing of the sort."

Shaking my head, I leave the bedroom and return to the kitchen, the glamorous knight in tow. "Special effects have come a long way over the years," I say, searching for something that resembles an unfamiliar techy gadget. "I know that aeggling wasn't real."

Shawn clears his throat. "If he was not real, then how did he toss about your cooking utensils." He gestures to the mess of pots and pans on the floor.

"Good point." I stare at the disaster, then at the helmet sitting on my counter. "So, if all of this is real, how did you get here?"

He shrugs. "The Sacred Text called to me for protection."

"Protection from what?"

"The aeggling of course," he replies. "Then I suppose, from you as well." Shawn's eyes narrow.

"From me? What could I possibly do? I love Oathbound; I would never do anything to ruin it."

The knight is quiet, pondering my words, then his expression brightens as if he's had a revelation. "Then the text in your private chambers must not be the original, merely a copy."

Light dawns on me. "Of course. My first copy, the one that was signed, was destroyed in the flood."

Shawn gasps. "No! Tell me it's not true." He drops to his knees with a clatter of metal against the kitchen floor. "Please, tell me you did not dispose of such a powerful treasure?"

Why are knights so damned dramatic in real life? "No, not yet. I have it tucked away." The copy meant so much to me I couldn't bear the thought of throwing it out. Not yet, at least. Maybe once the stench of must increases.

The knight stands. "Where is it? We must get to it before the aeggling, otherwise he will damage it further, forever merging our worlds." Shawn moves toward me, grabbing my hand. "Oh, beautiful Oath Master... I mean, just Ava... please help me protect the

Sacred Text to save both our worlds." He smiles, revealing a set of dimples that melts my heart.

"Yes, of course." My cheeks flush as I pull my hand from his and shake off the bizarre sensation of being attracted to a storybook character. "Follow me."

Shawn bows and then follows me to the basement stairs.

Flicking on the light, I lead him down to the almost dried-up laundry room. On top of a shelf across from us lay the original Oathbound copy, open to air dry. I point to it.

Aeggling screeches pull our attention to the left of the shelf, where the little bugger is jumping up and down, trying to get to the book.

"You there!" Shawn shouts, drawing his sword. "Halt!"

The creature screams, making both of us clutch our ears. When the wretched sound stops, Shawn charges towards the aeggling, making it turn and run through the basement. Cornered beneath a window, the creature growls, which reminds me of a lion cub, then vanishes once more. Shawn turns and rushes toward the book, just in time for the creature to appear on top of the shelf next to it.

"No!" Shawn calls out, swinging his sword, bringing it down upon the creature.

The aeggling evaporates into a purple cloud, sparkles falling on top of the shelf.

"Ha-ha!" Shawn says, clearly proud of his success. "He has been returned." He sheathes his sword and inspects the book. "It is greatly damaged."

With a sigh, I nod in agreement. "It was a terrible accident. I never should have left it in a box on the floor."

He touches a page and shakes his head. "Do you have a way of drying the pages? It may help to seal the portal?"

That explains how they got here. The water damage must have created the *portal,* or whatever. An idea comes to mind. "Yes, I have a blow dryer upstairs in the bathroom."

His eyes wide, Shawn smiles at me, his dimples appearing once more. Carefully, Shawn closes the book and picks it up from the shelf. "Lead the way, Oath Master."

What a ridiculous title, but I could get used to it. "This way, sir knight," I say with a bow, then lead him upstairs and down the hallway to the bathroom. Hopes high, I plug in the blow dryer and, one page at a time, we work away at drying them.

Reaching the last page, I glance at Shawn, who appears a little zoned out. "Are you alright?" I ask him.

Slowly, he looks at me. "I can feel the change. The portal between our worlds is losing strength. Soon, I will be gone from your land." He reaches out and takes my hand. "May I kiss you goodbye?"

Kiss me? A stranger in my home, acting like a drama king, wants to now... kiss me? I blink and stare at him for a moment. What harm could it do? He isn't a bad-looking dude, and it's not like I'd ever see him again. "I suppose so." I lean forward, eyes closed, waiting for his lips to find mine. Instead, he lifts my hand, and a damp, yet gentle, embrace touches the back of it.

"Thank you," Shawn says, releasing my hand.

That's all he wanted, to kiss the back of my hand? I fight back the laugh that threatens to escape my lips. I wouldn't want to offend the knight, after all. Time for the final page. "Are you ready?" I say.

Shawn bangs on his chest. "As ever."

It doesn't take long to dry the page, and I watch as Shawn slowly fades away, a smile on his lips. For a while, I stand there in awe, amazed by the magical night, with one hand on the now dry copy of Oathbound. I turn back to the opening, where the smudged signature stares back at me. If only it hadn't been destroyed.

A glow brightens the title on the page, and the ink recedes, reforming the original signature by the author.

I can't believe it! The book is almost fully restored, aside from water damage on the cover and the pages are a little crinkled up. I guess I can return the new copy and use the money to buy more books!

With a smile, I pick up the beautiful book and head into the kitchen. Sitting on the counter is the knight's helmet, right where he'd left it. I set the book on the counter next to it and place one hand on the cold metal. I will never forget the short time we had together, as dramatic as it was.

The next day, I return the second copy of the book and use the money towards a protective case that fits both the original copy and the helmet. In my bedroom, I mount it on the wall across from my bed, so that every night I'll think of Shawn and the scraggly little creature who once disturbed my sleep.

The End

The Wish in a Box: Part Two

Rebecca Hunnie

"Mom," Carla shouts as her eyes pop open, and she searches to see which room she is in. The box lay open on the floor, the quote resonating in her mind: *Do not wish to be anything but what you are and try to be that perfectly.* She is back home at her mom's. Getting out of bed, Carla looks through the house for her mom but cannot find her. Outside, the car is not in the driveway.

When she returns to her room a short time later, she searches her bed for her phone. When she hears a *Ding*, she pulls back the covers and picks up her phone to read a message from Alexis. * Party tonight at Sienna's, pick you up at 7? ~A~*.

*Sure. * That was all she wrote back.

Getting a bowl for breakfast, she looks at the date on her phone. April 17th, 2020, 7:45am. She is back in her time, just as confused as when she left. The box must have been the answer; her way in and out. Rushing back to her room, she finds it right where she left it earlier, in two pieces on the floor. Picking up the pieces, Carla realizes it's time to get ready for school. She doesn't want her mom more upset.

The bus picks her up outside, and she rides to school with her AirPods in. Her playlist roars to life in her ears with Morgan Wallen's Last Night, bringing memories of dancing with her best friends.

When she arrives at school a short ride later, Sienna and Trevor greet her, who are waiting for her in the bus loop. As a light drizzle comes down, Sienna greets her first.

"Morning, sunshine, heard you were grounded?" Sienna chuckles.

"You did?" Carla says sarcastically.

"Does that mean you won't be at my party?" she asks, rolling her eyes.

"Of course I will!" Carla says, excited.

"How? Won't your mom go postal?" Trevor says with a snicker.

"You let me worry about my mom," Carla cackles loudly.

"Great, see you later!" Trevor says, walking away as Sienna grasps Carla's arm firmly.

"What's up, Enna?" Carla asks, noticing the grasp from her friend.

"We need to talk," Sienna says, as they sit on a bench nearby.

"What is it?"

"What are you wearing to my party?" Sienna finally lets out a smile.

"Hadn't really thought about it."

"How could you not know? This is the biggest party of the year!" Sienna announces proudly, "Everyone is coming!"

"Don't we say that every week?" Carla says, letting out a booming laugh.

"What crawled up your tailpipe?" Sienna snaps with a sideways glare.

"Nothing, why do we make such a big deal about these parties when we always get blasted after?"

"Blasted?" she asks with sadness in her voice.

"In trouble, you know you are going to get into so much trouble," Carla says. "Your parents hate when you throw parties, which is why you haven't been able to have one in so long."

"Whoa, what is your deal? All I wanted to know was what you were wearing. If I had wanted a lecture, I would have told my parents about the party." Sienna stalks off in a huff.

She will cool off, Carla thinks to herself, as she notices Alexis getting out of her dad's car.

"Lexi." Carla runs up happy to see her friend.

"Whoa, hello!" Alexis says, embracing Carla with a hug.

"I am so happy to see you. I mean this you!" Carla says, squeezing her tightly.

"What are you rambling about?" Alexis says. "You're suffocating me!" She takes a step back, laughing. "Dude, we just talked this morning," she laughs.

As they walk to class, Carla is relieved that everything seems normal. She thinks to herself, *I will explain to her later why I am acting this way. I just want to take in being back here where life makes sense.*

"Dude, I just got a weird message from Enna. Did you talk to her this morning?" Alexis asks curiously.

"Yes, she asked me what I was wearing tonight?" Carla says. "We talked about clothes, and then she stormed off."

"She says you went off on her about how she will get in trouble," Alexis adds, rolling her eyes.

"You know Sienna; she is always so dramatic. All I asked her was why she was so excited when she knew she was going to get in trouble." Carla rolls her eyes.

"Carla, you need to be careful; Sienna is dealing with some stuff," Alexis explains cautiously.

"What, she never said anything." Carla pats her friend's arm.

"She didn't tell anyone. Please, just take it easy on her," Alexis pleads.

"Okay, I just don't understand what the big deal is. It was a joke?" Carla defends herself.

"Did you mention her parents?" Alexis asks her friend.

"Yes, but seriously, it was a joke," Carla snaps back defensively.

"Her parents are getting a divorce; she is taking it very hard." Alexis's voice is stern.

"What, she never said anything. Why didn't she tell me?" Carla questions with sadness in her voice.

"She knows how hard your parent's split was on you."

"I would be the one person who would understand," Carla says sullenly as they arrive at their first class.

The day flies by as both girls get a ride home from Alexis's dad. Carla gets out at home and rushes in the door to see her mom and dad at the table in the kitchen.

What's going on? Carla thinks to herself.

"Carls, can you come here, please?" her dad calls from the kitchen.

"I'll be right there," Carla shouts from the front door.

Entering the kitchen, Carla sees her mom standing near the stove, away from her dad.

"What's up?" Carla asks, locking eyes with her dad.

"Carla, your mom called me this morning from work. She says you ditched school yesterday and were being cheeky?"

"You called Dad?" Carla shouts at her mom.

"Do not raise your voice at her!" her dad interjects.

"Take it easy; it was just gym class," Carla snaps back quickly.

"Take a seat; we have some things to discuss," her dad says calmly.

Taking a seat, Carla and her parents discuss her behaviour and her attitude changes.

"I was coming home to tell Mom how happy I was to be back home," Carla says.

"Really?" her mother says sarcastically.

"Yes, yesterday was a wake-up call. I never should have said what I said, but I was mad that you grounded me." Carla stands to hug her mom.

"What do you mean?" her mom questions her as they hug.

"You would think I was crazy," Carla says. "Dad, was that the only reason you came over here, was to yell at me?"

"I wanted to tell you both, I met someone," he announces.

"Let me guess, her name is Ana?" Carla says with a grin.

"How did you know that?" her father says as Carla sits down and giggles.

"You will think I am crazy!" she repeats.

"No, really, how did you know her name?" he asks again.

"Let me guess; tall, blonde, average size and laughs at all your jokes?" Carla laughs loudly as her parents look at her confused.

"Carls, what's so funny?" her mom asks.

"It doesn't matter, am I still grounded?" Carla says.

"Your father and I have been talking, and it seems I may have overreacted. I want you to make up that testing, but we agreed the grounding is unnecessary right now. We just want you to try harder in school." Her mother stands and hugs her.

"That's great, so can I go to Sienna's tonight?" Carla says quickly, releasing from her mom's firm grasp.

"Really, not even twenty minutes ungrounded and you want to leave?" her dad asks quickly.

"Sienna is going through something, and I want to be there for her," Carla lies. "Alexis will be there too."

"We need to know things are going to change," her mom says, concerned.

"Change? What do you mean?" Carla asks with a raised brow.

"Your attitude, the way you speak to me and ditching school. It all needs to change. Can you do that?" her mom says.

"Sure, Mom, of course I can." Carla shrugs, brushing her mom's genuine concern off with sarcasm.

"That is what we are referring to; you can't just disregard what we say to get what you want. Do you understand?" her dad says sternly with his arms crossed.

"Yes, now can I go?" Carla attempts to leave the room slowly.

"Carla Hope-" her mom begins, but Carla cuts her off quickly.

"Mother..." Carla snaps, still walking backwards out.

"Just go... Get out...!" her mother sneers in anger.

"See you," Carla says, turning on foot before her dad can respond.

Carla heads down the hall to her room, where she glances at the box on the floor. She kicks it out of the way so she can get ready for Sienna's. There is a knock at her door. "What?" she shouts through the closed door.

"What is going on with you?" her dad asks, entering her room slowly.

"I am just so sick of her rules," Carla shakes her head.

After a long conversation with her dad, Carla finishes getting ready for Sienna's. She looks down for the box, but it has disappeared. Settling on a short purple mini and a white halter with a jean jacket, she puts her boots on to wait for Alexis. In the kitchen, her mom sits alone at the table, visibly torn, while sipping from a tall glass containing a clear fluid.

"Mom, I am leaving now," Carla announces.

"Get out if you don't want to be here — just go." Her mom wags her finger in the air, clearly intoxicated.

"Wow, okay. Goodbye, mother." Carla storms out in tears. *Wow, I definitely thought she would have cooled down by now,* she thinks to herself.

As she approaches Alexis's dad's car, she wipes her eyes and hops in the backseat with her best friend.

"Are you alright?" Alexis asks her.

"I don't want to talk about it," Carla says, leaning into her friends' open arms.

"Okay, I am here when you are ready." Alexis strokes the side of Carla's face gently.

"I know." Carla inhales deeply, trying to calm her nerves. The girls head to Sienna's without another word. Carla is still not ready to talk about what happened at home when they arrive and instead tells her friends she just needs a moment, so she heads towards the couch.

"What's her deal?" Trevor asks at the front door as Carla walks by, handing her jacket to him in silence.

"Her mom," Alexis says. "I think she didn't really say much. I wanted to give her some space. She will come out of it soon. Where's Enna?" She asks Trevor as she enters the foyer.

"She hasn't come down yet?" Trevor says, placing the girls' jackets in the nearby closet.

On the couch, Carla sits alone. Next to her sits a soft brown pillow. Grabbing it, she squeezes it and thinks to herself. *I can't believe she told me to get out. What did I even do?* A tear rolls down her face as Sienna comes down the stairs.

"What's your deal?" Sienna asks Carla, taking a seat next to her on the sofa.

"Nothing, I am fine. You look great!" Carla says, not wanting to spoil Sienna's night. "Listen, about earlier, I am sorry," Carla adds as they hug it out.

"Thank you, I really appreciate that. Now, let's get this party started." Sienna says getting off the couch to crank the tunes.

Sienna, Trevor and Alexis all dance around the floor as Carla remains seated on the couch.

Carla looks under the coffee table to see something sparkly. Reaching for the item, she pulls out a small purple sparkly box. *This again!* She opens the box.

There's a flash of light, and a loud bang wakes her. As she tries to adjust to the light in her room, she hears her mom shout.

"Carla, are you alright?" her mom calls from downstairs.

"Now where am I?" she asks, looking for a mirror. "Whoa!" Pigtails and overalls stare back at her.

"Carla, are you okay?" her dad shouts this time.

"Fine!" she yells back so they don't come in.

Looking in the mirror, she realizes she can't be more than 5 or 6. Looking for her phone, she digs through her bed and comes up empty. "Dad, have you seen my phone?" she asks him through the door.

"Phone, are you crazy? You are 6 years old; what would you need a cellphone for?" he chuckles, peeking in her door.

"Right, thanks, Dad!" she calls back, rushing to her desk where a calendar rests.

*April 24, 2010 * the date reads.

How on earth did I go back? I was just at Sienna's party, Carla thinks to herself with no memory of where she was before.

"Carla, honey, are you ready to go to Sienna's party?" her mom asks her.

"Party?" Carla asks, confused.

"Birthday party at the bowling alley?" her dad adds.

"Oh yeah, that, I just need a few moments. Is that okay?" Carla asks politely.

"Sure, sweetie!" her parents say in unison.

Wandering around her room, unsure of how she got there, she takes out a notebook and doodles. She hears her mom and dad talking in the kitchen.

"We said we wouldn't tell her yet," her mom says to her dad.

"We need to tell her soon," her dad responds. "We can't keep living like this."

As Carla finishes doodling, she remembers she needs to get ready for Sienna's party. "What do I wear to go bowling?" she giggles to herself.

"Carla, sweet girl, are you ready?" her mom asks through the door.

"Just about mom!" she shouts.

Carla heads out with her parents to the bowling alley, and she can't help but let her little mind wander. *What are Mom and Dad hiding? I bet it's a gift!*

Arriving at the bowling alley, Carla's dad gets out with her as her mom takes off, something that rarely happens. "That was odd. Why isn't Mom coming in?" Carla asks.

"She just has some errands to run." He shifts his gaze away from hers.

"Daddy, are you and Mommy keeping a secret?" she asks.

"Peanut, I want you to go have fun with your friends, alright?" he replies.

"Sure, Daddy!" she responds, heading off to be with her friends.

Bowling ends after presents and cake. A rousing chorus of Happy Birthday and lots of hugs. Carla and her dad wait outside for her mom to come. "Daddy, where is Mommy?" Carla asks.

"I am sure she is just running late," he says. "Carla, would you ask Alexis's dad to come here, please?" He gestures for her to go inside.

"Sure, Daddy!" Carla announces, excited to help her dad.

Alexis's dad comes outside and talks with Carla's dad. A while later after the party is cleaned up, Alexis's dad gives Carla and her dad a ride home.

"Daddy, can Alexis come in?" she asks her dad.

"Not tonight; it has been a busy day."

"Okay, Daddy," she says, hugging her friend goodbye.

"Bye, Carls!" Alexis says.

"Bye, Lexi," Carla calls back as her friend drives off with her father.

Inside the house, her mom sits at the table. "Daddy, how come Mommy couldn't pick us up?" she says.

"Mommy isn't feeling well," he replies.

"I feel fine," her mother slurs from the kitchen.

"Honey, why don't you go watch T.V. in your room? You can have twenty minutes before bath time!" He smiles with encouragement.

"Sure daddy! Thank you!" Carla rushes off to her room. After a while, she can hear her father shouting at her mom. She turns her T.V up as she typically does when they are loud.

A few moments later, her dad enters and says, "Bath time, pumpkin!"

"Yay!" Carla giggles, running towards him.

Bath time is met with a quick hair wash and playing with toys. When her dad leaves the bathroom, Carla continues to play on her own.

A short time later, her dad announces, "Bedtime!"

"Five more minutes?" she pleads with a smile.

"Sweetie, it is already past your bedtime. You have kindergarten tomorrow," he reminds her.

"Oh, right!" she says, tapping her forehead with a giggle before raising her arms towards her dad. "I forgot!" She adds with a smile.

Helping her out of the tub, her father wraps a towel around her and dries her hair. A crash rings out from the kitchen area. Her dad stops and asks her to go to her room, assuring her he will be right there, before taking off to the kitchen.

"What is wrong with you?" she hears her father shout. Carla peeks out her door and sees her dad carrying her mom to their room. A while later, her dad comes back. "You got yourself all ready for bed?" he asks with a kiss to her forehead.

"Can we read a story?" she asks him, pointing at the bookshelf nearby.

"Sure, how about this one?" he takes a book off the shelf, tucks her in and takes a seat next to her bed.

"I love you, Sweetie!" he says, kissing her forehead goodnight.

"I... love... you," she stammers out through tired eyes. Her father exits her room, and as he claps, the lights turn off.

The next morning from down the hall, Carla sees her mom is at the kitchen counter getting things ready for her lunch and work. She packs Carla's bag and puts it off to the side. "What happened to you last night?" her father snaps as he comes out of their bedroom, beside Carla's.

"Don't start." Her mom shouts back as Carla rushes back to her bed to pretend she is asleep, as she has done many times before. Not long after, her father knocks on the door and peeks inside. "Sweetie, it is time to get ready for school," he says, slightly shaking her shoulder.

"Daddy, is it morning already?" she asks.

"Yes, it is time to get ready for school. I will be dropping you off today!" he says before leaving.

"Yay, Daddy's big car today!" she jumps out of bed, excited.

Back in the kitchen, her mom takes off before saying goodbye. The door slams shut, the tires screech loudly, and she pulls out of the driveway in a huff.

"Daddy, where is Mommy?" Carla asks upon entering the kitchen.

"Whoa, you got ready fast!" her dad says with a jolt as she comes up behind him.

"School, I want to go to school," she says.

"You need to eat first," he says, passing her a bowl of cereal.

A while later, her dad buckles her into his vehicle, and they take off to her school. "Have a good day!" he says, kissing her cheek goodbye.

"Bye, Daddy!" she says, hugging him.

The day flies by, and Carla is excited when the office calls her to let her know she gets to go to Alexis's today.

When her dad picks her up later, she once again asks, "Where is Mommy?"

"Mommy still isn't feeling well." He looks away from her.

"Okay, are we going home?" she asks from the back seat.

"I thought we could have a dinner date. What do you think?" he says.

They arrive at McDonald's, Carla's favourite place to be. "Daddy, really?" Carla bounces in her seat.

"Let's do it!" he says, parking his deep red Chevy truck.

Carla plays on the play structure as her dad munches on French fries. Often looking back at her dad, she continues playing as kids come and go. Coming to have a bite to eat, she notices her dad's sad face. "Daddy, what is wrong?"

"What do you mean, peanut?" he asks her.

"You look sad."

"Could you go play? I am okay, sweetie. Thank you for asking," he tells her, and she rushes off to play.

A little while later they leave, and Carla hums in the back seat. At home, her dad helps her out of her seat. "You good, sweetie?" he asks as she hops out.

"Let's go, Daddy!" she tells him, rushing inside.

In the house, Carla's mom sits at the table. "Where... have... you... been?" she stutters loudly.

"Mommy, what's wrong? Daddy says you aren't feeling well, so he took me to McDonald's for dinner! We had a great time!" Carla says excitedly.

"Go... to... your... room..." her mother snarls incoherently.

Carla cries as she runs to her room. "Mommy is mean!" She slams her door.

"What is wrong with you!?" he yells loudly from the kitchen.

"Buzz off," her mom snarls at him.

"I can't do this anymore; I will tell Carla tomorrow that we are separating," her father says.

"Yeah, walk away, coward," she snarls at him. "Good luck taking my daughter from me. She will stay with me. I will make sure of it." She slams her cup on the table.

"We will see."

Carla hears footsteps down the hall.

"Daddy, why is Mommy so angry?" she asks her dad when he enters her room.

"Not now, sweetie, let's get you ready for bed," he says, stroking her hair gently.

"Okay, Daddy!" she agrees, giving him a hug.

Her mother comes into her room as they are reading a story together. "Get away from her; let me do that." She stumbles onto the bed.

"No, you need to leave. She is almost asleep." Her dad demands coldly.

"I can read her a book," her mother argues, as her dad takes her arm and directs her out of their daughter's room.

"Don't touch me!" her mom shouts at him.

"Please don't fight," Carla pleads, half asleep.

Her dad takes her mom by the arm and leads her toward the hallway. As they are walking out of the room, Carla hears her dad's angry voice. "There, are you happy?" He shuts off the light, leaving the door open a crack.

"Oh, come off it," she sneers. "You poisoned her against me; but you will never take her from me."

"I do not want to take her, but you are not making this any easier on any of us. We need to talk to her soon, and you need to be sober when we do. We do not want anymore outbursts like tonight. Is that clear?" Carla's father shouts as Carla pulls the covers up over her face.

"Leave me alone!" her mother demands. That was the last thing she heard.

As silence fills the air in Carla's room, she can fall fast asleep. The next morning is much like the last. Carla gets ready with her dad, and her mom is nowhere to be found. "Daddy, are you and mommy, okay?" she asks quietly.

"Sweetie, can you get ready?" he asks as she hops off her bed.

"Sure, Daddy!" she says, careful not to push him.

Getting ready for the day, sadness overwhelms her. *I wish Daddy and Mommy wouldn't fight.* Sitting on the floor, she peeks under her bed and is enchanted to find a small sparkly box. Gripping the box, she leaps back onto her bed.

"Carla, are you ready to go?" her dad yells from the kitchen.

"Yes, I will be right there, Dad!" she says, shoving the box aside.

Rushing to the kitchen, she finds her dad has a bowl of cereal ready for her again. She eats in silence to avoid upsetting him. Getting cleaned up, her dad says Sienna asked for her to go to her place after school. He buckles her into the truck.

"Yay!" she says excitedly. "Two days of playdates!"

Arriving at school, she sees a familiar face. "Daddy, Mommy is here!" she tells her father excitedly.

"Honey, what do you mean?" he asks, looking out his window.

"She is over there by the tree!" Carla says, pointing to a tree across the lot.

Carla and her dad drive closer to the tree. "Please stay here," he tells her.

"Okay, Daddy!" She says, remaining in her seat.

Her father gets out of the truck and approaches his wife. Carla can't hear what is being said, but her dad looks upset, and her mom storms off a short time later. Her dad returns to the truck and announces that they are going to have a daddy/daughter morning.

"Yay!" she says, excited, as her dad drives away from the school.

They arrive back at home, and her mom meets them. In the house, her mom is in the kitchen sipping on a glass of clear fluid. Her dad walks up and takes a sniff of the glass and goes to dump it out. "Carla, can you go to your room for a moment?" her father asks. "I need to speak with Mommy."

"Daddy, what about-" she says, as her dad glances at her.

"Soon, sweetie, we will go very soon," her dad cuts her off, guiding her with a gentle hand towards her room.

She turns on her T.V and turns up the volume. Her dad never lets her come home to watch T.V.

From her room, Carla can't quite make out what's going on. She turns down the volume on the T.V. and peeks out her door. Still unable to hear, she sneaks down the hall and slips into the pantry, her hiding spot.

"Celeste, I wanted so much more for you," he says to her kindly.

"Oh, please, you just want to take Carla," her mom says. "Look, you pulled her out of school to-"

"I pulled her out of school so we can talk to her. I hoped you would be able to stay sober, seeing as it is 9:40 am and a Tuesday. It's become apparent that your booze is more important. We need to talk to our daughter, and what do you do first? You chug a bottle of vodka and impair your mind. Do you even want us here?"

"You can't take her; she is all I have," she argues incoherently.

"You need help, and I can't keep doing this," her father explains.

"Get out then!" her mother shouts.

"No! We are going to talk to Carla. She is a brave young girl, and I know she will understand why this must happen now."

"No!" her mother replies. "We can't do this today. She won't understand," her mother snarls.

"I have wanted to do this for weeks. Every time we say we are going to talk to her, you start drinking and I let it go. I can't anymore. She doesn't deserve to see you like this."

"Fine, poison her against me so I am left alone," her mom says as Carla comes from the bathroom to hug her mom.

"Mommy, why are you crying?" Carla asks her mom.

"Carla, can you come over here please and take a seat?" her father says, directing her to the table.

"Daddy, what is going on?" she says, taking a seat between her parents.

"Carla, sweetie, this hasn't been an easy decision, and I know it won't make much sense to you right now; your mom and I will be living in different homes soon," her dad explains. "We will not be husband and wife anymore."

"But you will still be mommy and daddy, right?" Carla asks, her voice filled with sad whimpers.

"Sweetie, no matter where I live; I will always be your mommy," her mom says through slurred words.

"I will always be your daddy!" he chimes in.

"But you won't both be here to tuck me in?" Carla asks with tears streaming down her face.

"Now look what you did, Travis," her mom says before adding, "You... made... her... cry."

"Celeste, enough," her father snarls. "Carla, sweetie, we may not both be here to tuck you in, but we will always love you, and we will tuck you in separately when you are with us. Some days you will be with Mommy and some days you will be with Daddy, but we need you to remember something. Can you do that?" he asks her, kneeling down, so he is face-to-face with her.

"Daddy?" her voice is still filled with sadness.

"Remember, we will always love you, no matter what!" her dad says, hugging her tightly. "Please don't cry, my girl," he adds, holding her close.

"May I go now?" Carla asks quietly.

"Of course," her dad replies as she gets up and walks towards her room.

Once in her room, she sits on her bed and holds a squishy pillow close. *I wish we were all happy.* Carla glances at her closet.

Noticing a purple sparkly box, she gets down off her bed and walks toward it. Opening the lid, she cries harder. She returns to her bed and sits with the box on her lap, hugging it tightly. "I wish we were all happy again," Carla repeats to herself out loud. Placing her head on her pillow, Carla claps off her lights and closes her eyes.

Waking up, Carla opens her eyes, searching for her parents. She looks in the mirror and sees herself at 15 years old again.

"Carla Hope Erickson! Get down here!" her mother shouts.

The words echo in her head like a dream this time. "Talk about déjà vu," she says to herself. "I will be right there, Mom!" she shouts back.

Carla has come back to where she started, and she gets a do-over with her mom. She has seen where it could go and where it all started, and now, she has a chance to fix things before it's too late. Going downstairs to the kitchen, she hugs her mom. "I am sorry, Mom; I will try to be better. I love you so much!" She embraces her confused mom as they sit down to talk.

Counting her blessings on being back in her time, she finally admits to herself, *nothing is worth losing what I have.* The quote from the box returns to her mind: *Do not wish to be anything but what you are and try to be that perfectly.*

The End

The Others

Eric McKinnon

"Ya, they're patchin' this guy up now. I'm at the hospital. Nothin' serious. Say, Bill, how about that job for my boy..." Jeff Harris lit up one of his forever cigarettes as he barged through the front door of the little northern town's hospital, practically elbowing an elderly man out of his way as he did so.

"Hi, Jeff. How's the big engineer today?" The greeting came from one of the business moguls that owned half the town.

"Well, we're doin' dam good, ya might say. This is gonna be my pride and joy. When you're talkin' megawatts and makin' the Nelson work for ya, well, what can ya say."

"I guess. Well, we'll see you, Jeff."

"Not if I see you first." He laughed a rare laugh. And so did the businessman... laugh. When Jeff Harris laughed, everybody laughed.

Within minutes he tossed the cigarette butt into the closest snowdrift and quickly lit up again. With one good spit to the frigid air, he climbed in his car and was home just in time for supper.

"How was work today, Dear?"

"I told ya. Don't call me dear. Deer are good for nothin' but getting' shot. Where's that son of mine? 'Least suppose he's mine."

"Of course, he is Jeff," said his long-suffering wife.

"Just' kiddin', Rose," he said with a straight face.

"I know you're kidding."

"No, I ain't. It's jus' the way my dress hangs."

"Now, don't say that, Jeff, you shouldn't-"

"Shouldn't what? You afraid people might think I'm a girly boy?"

"No, Jeff. I just-"

"Pass me the spuds. Where is that kid anyway?"

"He had a meeting after school. The science club."

"Good for him. The more science, the better. How's that math mark?"

"I think it's up a bit."

"Ya think? Ya covering for him again? Dinner's great. Did ya defrost it yourself? Women got it so easy nowadays. Makes me sick."

"Now, Jeff, don't start. I have feelings too. And you shouldn't – oh, there's the door; Kim's home."

"Kim, for God's sake; I shoulda never let you give him a girl's name."

"It can be either, and you know it, Jeff. Hi, Kim."

"Ya, we hired a new guy today. His name's Petunia," he snarled, as he gobbled down a mouthful of potatoes.

"Hi, Mom," Kim shouted cheerfully, and then, not quite as cheerfully mumbled, "Hello, Dad."

"Umph."

"You know what, Dad?"

"No, can't say as I do."

"In the science club, we're starting to do all kinds of incredible things."

"Ya? Good for you."

"Mr. Jack says that he believes-"

"Mr. Jack. What kinda name's that?"

"Anyway, he says there's a strong possibility there is a fourth spatial dimension. And the reason we can't understand things were UFOs, and that is because we deny the existence of another dimension. Do you know what the 'wormhole' theory is about?"

"No, but I know what a dingbat is. Gimme that phone book. Jack, you say?"

"Dad, what are you-"

"Look. Your grandmother, you know how she went in her old age. How she babbled away about God knows what... 'other worlds' and stuff. I don't need you losin' whatever marbles ya got in your young age. The 'here and now', that's all there is. Ya, she kept saying the 'Others' would help me, help me live, I suppose. The doctor said she was delusional. In other words, she was nuts. Guy in my class said, "Your old lady's a loonie." I hadda punch him out. Hello, hello, speak up. Is this Jack? Ya, well this is Harris here. If you want to keep your job, no more fillin' Kim's head with garbage. What else ya do after school, ya got a crystal ball or somethin'. Goodbye."

"Dad, what are you doing? I've got to go to school tomorrow and-"

"So go."

Rose Harris finally broke into the conversation. "Jeff, you shouldn't have talked to Mr. Jack that way; he's a very nice young man. And he said on parents' night, that you never go to yourself, that Kim is a good student. Maybe you should-"

"Pass me the carrots, will you? The tooth fairy told me they're good for the eyes."

Later that evening, Jeff took up his usual spot at the local drinking establishment. After downing enough 'refreshment' to float the proverbial battleship, he returned home and, more or less, collapsed into bed. And fell asleep. Around three in the morning, there she was.

"Mom, leave me alone. I'm dreaming. I must be dreaming. Don't lecture me. I don't want to hear you. I don't want to... go like you, like what happened to you."

"Jeffry, you simply must listen to me. You cannot go on the way you are. The Others will help you as they helped me. Do as I say. You know you can trust me. Let them help. I will explain what you are to do."

Jeff, now unable to speak or move a muscle, did as she requested. He listened.

"Tomorrow night, there will be a whiteout, the likes of which even Churchill has never seen. You are to walk down to the traffic circle when the blizzard begins. When it intensifies, you won't be able to see one inch in front of your face. Do not be afraid. He is there to show you a greater reality. It will be pretty. And not pretty. He will speak of… choice. Do… do as I say, Jeffry."

He woke up in a cold sweat. Hungover, he, nevertheless, as per usual, arrived at the job site right on time. The day wore on. He fought to keep all thoughts of the previous night's dream from clouding his analytical mind. Steel was steel. Concrete was concrete. Mathematics was mathematics. Dreams were just that. Besides, he gladly observed, the sky was a beautiful turquoise, all of it, there was no wind, and the air temperature was actually quite tolerable.

A co-worker, another engineer, a Japanese fellow, who Jeff held a grudging respect for, arrived on the job for the afternoon shift. "Hello, hello, Mister Jeff. You hear the news?"

"News?"

"Enormous storm coming. May even have to shut down."

"Wha – what? But it's… a… lovely day."

"No, no. Weather office says it's a one in maybe five-hundred-year event. Look, look, the cloud… and it starts to snow…"

Early evening found Mr. Jeffy Harris standing alone in the centre of the town's traffic circle. No one questioned what was going on because there was no one around. The entire town was hunkered down in whatever buildings they considered safe.

His cell phone rang. "Jeff, why aren't you home? We're worried sick. Where are you anyway?"

"I'm okay. I'll be a little late."

"But where are you?"

"I'll explain later."

"Jeff, Mr. Jack called. He sounded really upset. You should phone again."

"Ya, I'll do that. 'Bye."

"I've got his number right here. Here we go. Jack? Harris again. Seems like you're causing me a lot of concern. Now, we wouldn't want anythin' to happen to you, now would we? Leave my kid alone with all that garbage. Or else."

The maelstrom morphed into the total whiteout that was... predicted?

Strangely, Jeff felt no fear. Or cold. Or... actually... anything.

Then came the voice.

"Take my hand. Walk forward with me. Leave the storm behind. Have no fear."

"Alright. Where am I? All these colours. This sweet music, this-"

"You are where you say you can't be. Because where you are does not exist according to you."

"You are..."

"I am... an Other. That's all you need to know. Behold." With that one word, the incredible panorama appeared. Past, present and future world events unfolded in vision after vision. Millions of scenes, that, incredibly, Jeff was able to process and completely assimilate.

"Why am I here?"

"You have just observed all the good and evil from the beginning of time. We've shown you it all. The men thrown to the lions, the nuclear attack on Japan, the Valentine's Day Massacre. Have I said enough? Listen well... there is no lower limit to depravity. Two dogs fight within every human being. Which dog gets stronger? The one you feed. Now, Jeffry, you must make a choice."

"No, no, don't try to convert me-"

"It's not what you think. We, the Others, only fit into a much larger plan. We only ask one simple thing."

"Which is..."

"We will return you to the circle. We do not ask you to say a hundred Hail Mary's or worship cows or even go to AA. All you must do, for the sake of your soul, for now, is to make a beginning. A first step. Start to deny evil and embrace good. Just... begin. Take that step."

"Or?"

"You will... not return to the circle."

"Alright. I will," he found himself muttering.

"Do not lie. We have certain powers..."

"I... will do as you say."

Minutes later:

"Jeff Harris, get in this house. What is going on?"

"I've got to phone Kim's teacher."

"Oh, God, Jeff, maybe you shouldn't. He says he might get the-

Hello, Mr. Jack. I'm calling to-"

"Look, Mr. Harris, I have the number of the RCMP right in front of me. If you-"

"No, no. Mr. Jack, I want to thank you for... all your service in the school. And if I can help in any way in the science club, I'd love to. And, as you are well aware, you guys are heavily subsidized... by us... and I'll try to use my influence to increase... increase... Mr. Jack, are you still there? Are you listening?"

Kim muttered to his mother, "What's... with him?"

After a moment of silence came the reply... "Yes, yes, Mr. Harris, sir... I'm... I'm listening..."

The End

Time Travel

Denise Fenez

When my grandfather passed away, amongst his earthly possessions was a journal written when he emigrated to Canada. This is my inspiration for this partly fictional story.

Journal Entry:

Today is Monday, May eighth, nineteen eleven. The harbour where the ship awaits me is in Le Havre, which can be translated as the Port. This is in the region of Northern France where I was born in eighteen eighty-seven in Cambresis, in a farming community near the Belgium border. I, Martial Leopold Fenez, am leaving my home in France, via a large ship which is destined for Canada. Maman is not in good health and could not come with Papa and brother Louis to see me off. They are happy that I am embarking on a great adventure.

Ever since I finished my compulsory conscription in the French army, Father Blondelle, our local priest, has been trying to convince me to emigrate to Canada. He told me that the Canadian government is offering one hundred and sixty acres of land free to qualified young men who want to farm on the prairies. This is called the Dominion Lands Act. The new immigrant must be prepared to build a residence and use at least five acres within ten years. This would not be difficult as a person could order a farm house through the Eaton's catalogue, and the house would arrive by train. All you need to do is pay for it and assemble. Everything needed is supplied in this kit. Father Blondelle offered to help me with the paperwork needed to emigrate. This began two years ago and now I am twenty-four years old and leaving for Canada.

From the deck of the SS. Rochambeau, I could see Pappa and Louis standing on the dock straining to see me amongst hundreds of people. I was waving, but so was everyone else. It felt like we were so close and yet so far from each other. That must be how a butterfly feels when leaving its cocoon. It was comfortable and safe then everything changed. The ship moved away and the people on the dock became smaller and they begin to disappear. The wishes of *Bon Voyage* faded away.

My trunk was put into storage and I would not see it until I disembarked in Quebec. It had taken me

weeks to pack as it was hard to decide what I would need. Pappa put some basic tools in the bottom of

the trunk such as a saw, hammer and a knife. He would have filled the whole trunk with tools if I had not

stopped him. Surely there must be some available in Canada, I would not be the only person there. Then

the decision on clothing must be made. I heard it gets quite cold there in the winter. Maman's friends

started knitting mitts, toques and sweaters for me. The V-neck sweater I am wearing today is a gift from

these wonderful friends. It was knit with wool that still had lanolin in it which made it waterproof. Back

to what is packed in the trunk. I had several books, but was limited as to how many would fit in my trunk.

My suit that I would need for going to church on Sundays. I added a few sets of work clothes and some

work boots. Maman prepared a mending kit for me with several needles and thread, scissors and

measuring tape. I had a suitcase for the trip, with a shaving kit, toothbrush, a bar of soap, a towel and

washcloth, two books, one pair of socks, one pair of underwear and cigarettes. Smoking was a habit

which started in the army. My next move was to find out how to get to my cabin. As it turned out third class was in the bowels of the ship right on top of the engine rooms. The cabin was very small, with the one set of bunk beds, one wash basin with a pitcher of water and a couple of chamber pots with lids. I understood some people might get seasick, making these very necessary. A formidable round window called a porthole allowed the small room to be illuminated with sunshine. The walls were painted white and the linoleum was salmon pink. On the inside of the door was a ship plan. A large dining room was centrally located where we would receive three meals a day at the time that we would be assigned.

There was a smoking room for the gentlemen and a games room for all to enjoy plus two sets of communal toilets, one for males and one for females and children. Bathing was a luxury, as seven hundred people shared two bathrooms, so a reservation was needed. A jug of hot water would be delivered to all cabins daily. For exercise, there were promenade decks and also deck chairs to sit and read. At the rear of the ship was the poop deck which was great for observation, as it was the highest spot on the ship.

I decided to choose the bed I liked best before my roommate arrived. The bottom bunk was my first attempt. The mattress was stuffed with straw, which felt okay. The top bunk had a good view from the porthole. I could watch ships sailing by. To mark my bed, I placed my suitcase on the top bunk. I heard a small knock on the door and my roommate entered. He was a young man dressed in a three-piece

tweed suit and wearing a Panama hat. I was impressed. I thought of the children's book *Country Mouse*

Meeting the City Mouse.

"So, we are going to be roommates," he said. "My name is Pierre. Mmm, not even a chair to sit on, let's go to the smoking room to get acquainted."

I pointed to the ship's plan taped to the door and told him that it looked like our assigned time to have dinner was seven pm. We had plenty of time to go and smoke a cigarette. I was dressed in wool tweed trousers, buttoned shirt with tie V-neck sweater and my Basque Beret. While we walked around looking for the smoking room I took mental notes. This was not going to be easy as the patterns kept repeating. Stairs, lifeboats, deck chairs. Pierre had not even looked at the ships plan. Suddenly I could see a group of gentlemen sitting in what looked like a beer parlour. That must be the smoking room. Now that was something I could relate to. We walked in and found a comfortable place to get to know each other. Pierre liked to talk so it was easy for me. I was not too talkative.

"So, which part of Canada are you going to?" Pierre asked.

Not even waiting for an answer he proceeded to tell me that he had just finished an accounting degree at a University in Paris. His uncle in Quebec has a job at the bank of Montreal waiting for him and he would be living with his uncle's family.

'*So why is he travelling third class*?' I wondered. Here I was going to the Prairies, not knowing what to expect, not knowing a single soul in all of Canada. As Pierre continued, he revealed more about himself. I had a sneaking suspicion that gambling might be a problem he struggled with.

Pierre asked, "where did you say you were going?"

"I am going start farming on the prairies"

"They say there are lots of savages in Manitoba" he said.

"They never told me," I replied, feeling a little indignant.

The bell rang reminding us that the next group could come to eat. "I sure hope it is good; I am starved, but I've got to go back to the room to wash up."

"Wait for me," Pierre said. We retraced our tracks and found our cabin.

After dinning on lamb ragout with hardtack and tea, we found our way to the poupe deck. What a sight. The sun was starting to set in the west. The sun would be the only navigation tool we would have for the rest of the voyage.

When we settled in our beds for the night, I could not help but wonder if what Pierre said about Manitoba was true. I was too tired to waste my time fretting. The boat rocked me to sleep.

The sun was shinning once again and our assigned breakfast was at seven am. They served us a watery porridge sprinkled with pieces of dried apple, accompanied with hardtack and tea. Unlike Oliver Twist, we could have more if we wanted. I went out on the deck to find a chair where I could sit and read my book. Pierre went to the games room to play some card games with like-minded men.

The morning went by quickly and it was time for a two pm lunch. This was a disappointment. I am not much of a cook but

I swear they just added water and barley to the ragout we had last night and called it soup. Of course, there was hardtack and tea. I did not see Pierre at lunch time; we did not have assigned seats. I spent the rest of the afternoon writing in my journal and walking along the promenade. I spotted several young ladies who smiled at me. There were a few groups gathered together enjoying some Irish folk songs. They sure looked like they were having a good time. I do not speak English so can not sing along, but sure enjoyed the music. The clouds began drifting overhead and the wind made the boat rock a bit more intensely. And it is time to eat again.

Can you guess what was on the menu for dinner? Lamb ragout! Hardtack and tea.

The weather was getting worse. I decided to head back to the cabin where I could lie down. The storm got continuously worse with thunder and lightening. I had not seen Pierre for most of the day, and I wasn't sure where he was now.

Then the wind blew the door open and Pierre stumbled in. "How is the old cowboy?" he asked and then continued "Boy, is this a storm, we had to stop playing cards and were told to head back to our rooms. They seem to think we might get washed overboard if this storm gets worse," he continued. "I feel sick."

"There is a chamber pot at the end of your bunk," I said, "Keep it handy."

I must have fallen asleep, but soon woke up to Pierre vomiting with a stench that made my stomach do summersaults. We were told to keep our porthole closed, but I could not do that. I turned in my bunk and reached over to open the porthole. I stuck my head right out the window to get some fresh air. The rain seemed to be moving sideways. The salty ocean water sprayed my face, and when the lightening lit up the sky I saw something coming at me that looked like a small tornado. Suddenly, I was sucked out of the porthole. I went into the sky being tossed and turned, not understanding what was happening to me. My clothes were ripped off. My mind was stripped as well. I did not know who I was. Then suddenly I was dropped into some fresh cold water close to shore. I barely had enough strength to climb the bank up into the trees. I found some clothing that fit me perfectly.

And then I remembered. I had just finished playing a game of Lacrosse with my cousins who were here for the spring celebration. Feeling so hot after the game I decided to go cool off in the water. I must have stayed in the water too long.

Am I hungry right now! Rushing to the longhouse, I met some of my friends heading in the same direction. The women had been preparing food for days now. We were given several smoked fish to eat as well as some unleavened corn bread. Fishing was something we did all year round. These fish were caught when the lake was covered with ice and then smoked. Once we had eaten our fish, we had to go into the forest to collect Fiddle Heads. The younger boys came with us. Fiddle Heads are the new shoots from the Ostrich fern and are only available in early spring. The other delicacy that awaited us was the sap of the Maple tree which had been collected a few months ago. We collected the sap but the women turned it into the most delicious, sweet treats. I was looking forward to our evening feast

Now we had to go and get some fresh water. This means quite a long walk to the place where the water is more turbulent and the water is fresher. As we walked along the shore our conversations drifted from the young girls that had changed so much since the last feast we had, to the new French men that had come to us wearing long black robes and having faces like dogs. I wonder, *why, they have hair covering their faces? They seem quite dumb as well. They would never survive if we did not feed them. Not knowing our language will make it difficult for us to teach them anything.*

After getting back and delivering our water to the women, we headed out with our bows and arrows to have some target practice. By the time we wandered back the meal was ready. We sat outside the longhouse, but the food was inside. The young women brought plates of food to the elders and guests. The plates were piled high with roasted moose meat, steamed fiddle heads sprinkled with sunflower seeds, wild rice and unleavened corn bread. After dinner we were offered some tea and sweet treats made with the maple sap. The women cleaned and the men sat around a fire smoking and catching up with the gossip. Once the women had finished and joined us, everyone stopped talking and the Chief began to speak.

"We are the proud people of the Huron nation. Our ancestors have been here since time began. Our territory is known as Turtle Island. We work hard and have survived many droughts, heat waves, fires started by lightning, and bitter winters. We have learned to overcome, but in the recent past we have had new challenges. The white men with hairy faces have come to Turtle Island offering us many gifts for the fur pelts we collect from the animals we kill for food. Axes, pots and pans, knives, the bright beads the women like. But now the Dutch are trading rifles. This has increased the number of animals being killed. The Iroquois have killed so many for trading that they need more territory to hunt. We hear of the wars to which our neighbours are being subjected.

We are a peaceful people and do not have the guns that the Iroquois have. We want to live in peace. Many of our people have been dying from strange illnesses. Our Shamen does not know what to do. When speaking with our neighbours we understand that the Iroquois do not like weak captives. If you show that you are afraid of them, they will kill you for sure, but if you are brave, they may adopt you to replace someone from their tribe who has died. We must keep our eyes and ears open; I will pass the talking stick around the circle and when everyone has had a chance to make suggestions we will go to bed for the night." The talking stick was passed around the circle but no one spoke. Maybe they were too tired or maybe they were deep in thought.

The next morning, we were awakened by the smell of fish being fried in one of those wonderful fry pans that the dog faces traded, unleavened bread being cooked on hot rocks and sweet tea to drink. The sun was shining and it looked like it would be a wonderful day. Everyone had certain jobs that must be done before we could play games. Water must be replenished, wood must be gathered, clothing washed, and all things prepared for another feast that night. The women were barking the orders. The entertainment would be story telling. The men travelled around Turtle Island trading with other tribes and they always came back with wonderful, exciting stories. After storytelling, the young men would learn how to drum, and the older men would allow some of the younger men join them.

The day had been filled with Lacrosse and other games. This had made us hungry. The women had prepared plenty of rabbit stew and corn bread which was available any time we wanted to eat. This feast was so much fun. As the day began to cool a bit, it was time to eat again. The women had been working all day while we were playing games. The outside oven had been busy roasting more moose and muskrat. That night, we had salad made with dandelion leaves, which was also a special spring treat. There was also squash that had been steamed and mashed, beans that had been cooked with spring onions and sweet honey cakes waiting for us when we brought back our plates.

The fire blazed and everyone sat in a circle. The men shared the tobacco pipe and waited for the women to join them. Once everyone was seated, the talking stick was passed around and the stories began.

The tall one said, "I learned what the Black Robes are doing when they are drawing in their books. He is tall, muscular and quite a ladies' man if he gets the chance. The Curious One in this village I visited had questioned the Black Robe. 'Why do you draw pictures all the time?' he asked.

'Let me show you' the Black Robe replied. He said this as he turned to a clean page in his book. The Black Robe asked him to share something that no one else knew. The curious man then proceeded to tell him about an embarrassing situation he had found himself in when he was a young man. 'I started a grass fire that spread and burnt our birch bark canoe.' The Black Robe was busy scratching in his book. When he was finished, he asked the Curious One to take the book to the other Black Robe who was at the waters edge watching the men fish. 'Ask him to look at it and then tell you what the book revealed,' he instructed. The Curious One was shocked to find out that the scribblings told the Black Robe what he had never told anyone until that very day." He passed the talking stick to Chubby with an air of confidence.

"On my travels I found out that a certain village had traded some of their furs for bed coverings that they called blankets. They are lighter than animal hides, but, since they started using the blankets, they have been getting sick, and many have died." He paused in deep thought for awhile then passed the talking stick to Tall Tales.

"I was hunting this past week with my bow and shot the bull which we have been enjoying. He was one big moose I tell you." Tall Tales passed the talking stick to his friend called the Smooth Talker.

"I heard that hunting has not been very good down south. The white men keep asking for more furs and our people want more trinkets, rifles, and now they are trading for a drink they call whiskey. The fur trader showed us how this whiskey can be set on fire. It is quite bitter but the taste does not reflect the way it makes you feel. I traded some of our honey for a bottle of this fire-water for us to try." Smooth Talker passed the stick on to the Quiet One.

"Not too far from here I found some strawberries. They are not quite ready yet, but it looks like a good year for berries." He passed the stick on. The next person had nothing to say. The stick kept moving.

It stopped at a serious young man called No Toes. He had frost bite when he was young and lost some of his toes and walked with a limp. "My news is not good. Our neighbours, not too far from here, were attacked by the Iroquois and many were killed, some tortured and some taken as prisoners. They left only the old people untouched. They tortured the Black Robes who were living in that village. They chopped off their ears skinned them alive and then killed them." We all sat in silence. The stick continued to move but no one spoke.

The stick returned to the chief. He stood and said, "it is time to dance, let us not worry about this now." The drummers prepared and the singing began to awaken a spirit within, and everyone danced. This lasted for hours. During this time, my friends dared me to find that bottle of fire-water and take a sip. Not wanting to turn down a dare, I slowly moved to where the bottle was sitting in plain view. The bottle had not yet been opened. While everyone was distracted, I took the bottle and ran toward my friends. They needed to watch me drink the firewater to prove that I was taking the dare. The water to refill the bottle was ready. I opened the bottle and took a very long drink, coughed, and took another sip. The bottle was filled with water and then returned before anyone noticed. After I felt very smug. It did not take long and I could feel everything swirling around me. I passed out. I could hear the women shouting, "he's dead, he's dead." The voices faded as I drifted into a deeper realm of consciousness.

When I became aware of my situation, I had a terrible headache and felt ill.

My roommate, Pierre, was watching me. "I am so happy to see you in the land of the living, cowboy. You have been sick and were hallucinating. You must be starved."

"No, I am not hungry, but I sure am thirsty," I replied

"You need to look outside and see the huge floating chunks of ice," said Pierre excitedly. Let's go sit out on the deck before the bell calls us for supper. You haven't missed much; we get lamb ragout every day."

I told Pierre that I would skip supper as my stomach was still upset. The ice was a fantastic blue colour. I had never seen such a sight before. I was so tired that I went to bed and slept like a baby.

I had no dreams, no nightmares, just a restful sleep.

The next day arrived and Pierre was anxious to tell me that we would be in Halifax that same day. We docked at the harbour and some passengers disembarked. We had to stay on the ship as we were going to the city of Quebec. I noticed them loading some provisions. Maybe we would have something different for supper. No such luck. We had lamb ragout, but we had biscuits instead of hardtack.

We were not in Halifax for a long time. Our journey continued to Quebec via the St Lawrence River. Being anxious to get off the boat, I walked up and down the promenades. Then, at last, we had arrived. We had to wait until the first class disembarked and then the second class and then it was our turn. Both Pierre and I had been ready for hours. I collected my trunk and made my way to immigration. We were told to wait in line. Finally, it was my turn. Thank God, the officer spoke French. He asked me what my name was and I told him Martial Leopold Fenez. He informed me that people here do not trust the Spanish. "From now on you pronounce your name like your nose, *nez*. Nay"

"Where are you going?" the officer asked.

I replied, "I am going to start farming on the prairies. I have all my papers here."

"Very good, let's see," questioned the officer. "Is it Saskatchewan or Manitoba?" He ruffled through the papers. "Okay, it looks like Winnipeg is your destination. That is in Manitoba. There is someone here that will take you to the train station to check in your trunk and find you a hotel for tonight. Your train leaves tomorrow at noon. Good luck Mr. Fenez." With a smile, he said, "Welcome to Canada."

The End

Gemstone: Part Two

Lasalina Tess

The village fades until it's no longer visible. I hold on to Roan with a sense of peace; riding nestled together on the back of a magnificent dragon over Calidora. It's like living the dream I've had since I was young and first picked up a Tolkien novel. Deciding to remain with Roan and Talon, at least for now, wasn't easy. Staying means being away from other humans, and if they find a way home, it also means remaining in this strange new world. Yet the thought of being parted from Roan is too much to bear. Our connection only grows the longer I'm with him. I'll never understand how it started.

What else will I encounter here? That a simple touch could create a powerful bond between strangers is intimidating. Once, I believed I had fallen in love, but as time passed, we agreed we were better as friends. This is different. Could this connection be the real thing? Is this spark the creation of an intimate flame, one that will consume me?

One day at a time. I repeat these words in my mind, knowing that Talon can hear every single word my thoughts generate. One day at a time.

We continue past our original campsite, the place where Roan found me, and onwards to the west. Trees appear taller here, making Talon fly higher than before, yet I wish I could see more of this world than just treetops and distant mountains. Roan spoke of elf cities earlier. My gaze shifts to the points of his ears. As a child, I read stories of such creatures. One stands out above the rest: The Lord of the Rings. Is Roan like the elves created by the master of high fantasy, Tolkien?

The farther we travel, the older the trees look, with thicker trunks and taller than any I have seen. Talon soars lower, and Roan pulls my arms tighter around him, just in time for the dragon to dive between the trees. She turns sideways, her wings narrowing against her sides as we bob and weave between obstacles. If I reach out, the ground is almost within reach, but it gives me the creeps being so low and at this speed.

Finally, Talon levels out and lands, halting. Ahead is a small cabin built between two massive trees, one on either side. There are no refined planks for the walls, but logs which somehow mould together, reminding me of country log homes and cabins on Earth.

"Welcome to my home, Tara," Roan says. He turns in place and reaches down to unfasten me from the dragon's leather saddle blanket. With one hand around my waist, we slide off Talon's back, landing on the damp forest grass.

"I thought dragons lived in mountain caves," I say.

He chuckles. "Not this one. Talon prefers the Forest of the Ancients. The prey is much larger here."

I glance around the old forest, imagining massive bears and dire wolves sneaking in the shadows. Unless there are other, more fearsome creatures here. Ones that could gobble me up in one bite.

Roan removes the gear from Talon's back, and I follow him toward the cabin, where he tucks things away in a wooden chest next to the door. The sack filled with the fire-roasted boar is slung over his shoulder, and he gestures for me to enter the cabin.

Inside smells of freshly cut wood, apples and meat. A fireplace is set into the wall across from the entrance, beside which is a stack of logs ready for burning. There's no furniture; no table or chairs. Only a bed of furs lay stretched out across the floorboards.

"Did you build this place?" I ask, rubbing my arms from the chill that settled in the cabin.

Roan closes the door behind him and sets the sack against the wall. "Every bit," he replies. "I have little, but I need little." He kicks off his boots. "Mostly because Talon and I aren't around often."

Following his lead, I remove my runners but keep the fur around me for now. The flight was cold, and without a fire burning, so is the room.

He gestures to the bed. "Would you like to sit while I make us something to eat?"

With a smile and a nod, I cross the room and sit comfortably in the warm bed of soft furs, which are cool against my backside. If I make it home, how much would it cost to purchase one of these blankets? It would probably cost a fortune, but here, it's free. All you would have to do is kill an animal and skin it. A shiver rushes through me. I've killed nothing besides spiders or other creepy crawlers that have entered my home. Or fish, which Dad taught me how to clean properly.

Home: the place I long to see but cannot reach. What will happen if I'm stuck here? Will someone report me as missing? Are there security cameras at Jacob's Trading? They'd probably see a flashing light, then my body vanishing. I guess the bank would take possession of my house because there's no family in the area. I've never written a will or listed anyone as an emergency contact. Except that the hospital, which would be my best friend, Katrina. My bills will pile up, but who would pay them in my absence?

Roan starts a fire, then carries a wooden tray across the room and sits next to me. On it, is two apples, bread of some sort, and a container of jam.

"Looks delicious," I say. "What kind of jam is it?"

"Jam?" Confusion crosses his face. "Oh, you mean the berry spread."

I nod.

"I traded meat for it at the market near the main city. These berries grow northeast of the city by waterfalls."

The bread appears to be more filling than the apple, so I grab a chunk and smother it with the deep red jam and take a massive bite. A sweet flavour fills my mouth, and after swallowing it a tart aftertaste lingers. It reminds me of something I've tasted before, but I can't put my finger on it. Once we finish devouring every bite, I slide the furs off my shoulders, feeling warmed and my hunger satisfied. We wash it down with cool water from his satchel.

Roan sets the tray next to him on the floor, with only two apple cores remaining on top, and then he moves in front of me. With his legs crossed, he says, "What is it like on Earth?"

That's a loaded question. What to tell him first... "Well, there's many people, buildings. Vehicles and noise." I shrug. "Is there something specific you'd like to know?"

He smiles, quiet in thought for a moment. "What do people trade for goods?"

"Money. We make coins and paper bills. Which means everyone has to get a job and work for a living to pay for homes, gas, and food. Basically everything, including clothing."

Roan's smile vanishes. "The humans in the village do well with farming and hunting. Do you not do the same on Earth?"

I laugh. "Some people do, but me, personally? No. There are massive farms and companies that make products to sell in stores, like markets. So, I buy everything that I consume."

He shakes his head. "I can't imagine having to rely on others for food. Sure, some specialty items I trade for, like the berry spread, but most of my food I gather myself. Or Talon helps me hunt for it."

We remain quiet for a moment, both of us in our own thoughts. The differences between our worlds are vast, and I have a lot more to learn about Calidora. And dragons. Spending more time with Talon is forefront of my mind. Aside from Roan.

"What do you do for fun?" I say, breaking the silence.

He shrugs. "Live."

I blink, taking in that single word. "Do you have any hobbies?"

Roan glances around the room. "There isn't much time, but I would say flying with Talon and helping those we find along the way."

"Like, how you helped me."

Our gazes meet, and he smiles. "Exactly. This season alone I've found about a dozen humans wandering through the forest. One I located trapped on a cliff, shivering. The poor boy was young and terrified. When I brought him to Ben, the boy clutched him and refused to let go."

"What a thing to go through at such a young age," I reply. Imagine being eight years old and being sucked through a portal into a scary place, filled with unimaginable creatures, never to see your parents again. It makes me want to find that portal stone even more, but not for myself, for the young who have left their families on Earth. "Would someone at the market have one of these magic gemstones to help humans return home?"

The expression on Roan's face becomes sombre. "No." His gaze lowers.

I reach out and touch his hand. "If you were sucked away from your home against your will, would you not want to return? What if you were separated from Talon? Wouldn't you want to get back to her?"

With a sigh, he nods, then meets my gaze. "I don't like the thought of you leaving, though."

Guilt strikes me, and I reach out to touch his face. "I'm not leaving yet, Roan. Right now, I just want to be here with you."

The corner of his mouth lifts, a sideways grin on his face, but the smile does not reach his eyes. "Then we should go to the Guarri, where the portal first opened. If anyone knows if a portal gemstone exists, it will be them." A sadness still lingers in his eyes. "You should rest. The ride is long."

He stands, but I grab his wrist to stop him.

"Wait," I say. "Will you stay with me?"

Warmth spreads through my arm, and a feeling of anticipation fills me. It's as though his every emotion is being passed to me through touch.

Silently, Roan nods and slides next to me.

As I lay down in the bed of furs, Roan lowers himself next to me, his face across from mine. I try to keep my eyes closed, but I can't. We lay there, staring at each other.

Roan's hand rises and touches my cheek, his fingertips gently exploring the curve of my face. They reach my chin, then my lips; tingles spread across my skin. Like a moth to a flame, or a magnet to a fridge, our lips join in a passionate kiss. The room melts into nothingness. The crackle of fire becomes static noise in the background.

We slide closer together, pressing our bodies against one another, increasing the heat within my limbs. He's well-toned, but not over-done like a wrestler, and I can feel the strength he possesses. I ache for him, like I've never ached for anyone before. It's like my entire life has taken me to this moment. Roan slides a warm hand beneath my shirt, and I sit up to remove the obstacle.

"You want this?" he whispers. "With me?" Questions roam in his gaze.

"Very much," I reply. "More than anything."

One item at a time, we remove our clothing, and when our bodies merge, it's as though we've always been together in this way.

His passion is clear in the way he touches me and moves with me. Maybe it wouldn't be so bad to be stuck here with Roan.

Hot and sweaty, lying in Roan's arms amongst the furs, we drift off to sleep.

The rest of the day and evening we spend together, dozing off and on, enjoying each other, quenching our thirst. We agree to leave for the Guarri caves at nightfall, so that by morning we'll arrive there. Physically drained from our time together, I clutch onto Roan and admire the stars, but the wind and movement of Talon are like a lullaby as I drift off to sleep.

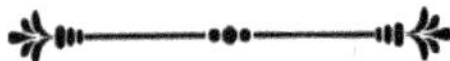

Sunbeams strike the backs of my eyelids, rousing me from an awkward sleeping position. The land below us has changed; the trees are smaller, young and vibrant. Rocks line hills, and ahead of us they rise into smaller mountains. Talon finds a safe place to land, which Roan says is only a walk away from the cave mouth we're looking for.

We dismount and embrace before off-loading a sack of supplies that Roan packed for our journey. Hand-in-hand, we walk through tall grass with hidden rocks, making me fumble often. The wind is gentler down here than flying through the Calidora skies. A sharp aroma rests heavy in the air: herbs and dirt. At the mouth of the hidden cave entrance, we stop and face each other.

"The Guarri speak their own language," Roan explains. "You may not understand our conversation, but I will share it with you once we finish."

"No problem, I understand," I reply, gazing into his beautiful hazel eyes. Memories of our naked bodies intertwined float through my mind, warming my core.

Roan leans down and kisses me, his tongue tangling with mine.

The sensation of being watched causes me to pull away from him. At the cave entrance, an odd-looking creature stares at us. Her skin is milky-green, with tendrils sticking outward from her cheeks like antennae would stand upwards on an animated alien. Only instead of two, there are three on either side of her face, and they appear to move and sway as she shifts her weight. She speaks, her voice mid-ranged and aggressive, as if she's angry.

Roan answers in a similar, unfamiliar language, using words I couldn't spell out on paper. When the Guarri answers, her tone is calmer. She returns inside the cave.

"What did she say?" I ask Roan.

"Humans may not enter the cave," he replies.

"What? What does that mean?"

He sighs. "It means we have to wait outside for the Overseer to come outside to speak with us." Roan moves to a large boulder, where he sits.

I join him. "Do they not trust humans?"

He shrugs. "I suppose not. They used to be allies, but now... I guess something changed that."

Great. It sounds like they'll be less likely to help humans find a way home. Not that I'm sure I want to leave. I slip my hand into Roan's, and he smiles.

We sit in silence until three figures emerge from the cave. One is the Guarri we met initially. Another is an old male Guarri who walks with a stick and a younger male who assists him. Once they are near, Roan and I stand to greet him.

The old Guarri examines us with his quizzical gaze, pausing at my face for a moment before fixating on Roan. He says something in his language, his voice hoarse from age.

Roan responds, then glances at me.

The old guy steps closer, gaze never leaving mine. "Child, you have come a long way to ask something of me," he says, speaking perfect English. "What is it you wish to ask?"

Briefly, I look to Roan for guidance, but he only nods encouragement. With a sigh, I look at the Overseer. "I was hoping you may offer the humans here... a way back to Earth. A portal stone, maybe."

The man laughs long and hard until he chokes on it. Once he catches his breath, he says, "Many have come before you to ask such a thing. Some have even died by our hands for forcing their way into our cave-home. This sparked our decision to ban all humans and increase our guards' watch-time. Never have we felt more threatened than by the humans of Earth."

Instinctively, I step backward.

Roan moves in front of me like a shield.

"Calm yourself, Roan," the man says. "We will not harm you unless provoked, for humans are the aggressors." Pure anger comes through in his voice. "You should choose better company."

Roan glances over his shoulder at me, then faces the Guarri. "You have yet to answer Tara's question," he says.

The Overseer shakes his head slowly. "If there were, we would have sent humans home years ago." He gestures to the female, who steps forward and takes an aggressive stance in front of us. Then, the Overseer and his companion return to the cave.

"Leave," the female shouts.

It must be the only word of English this Guarri knows. I tug on Roan's arm to encourage him to back down; his arm is tense, fists clenched. At last, he relents, and we walk in silence to where we left Talon, while the female's eyes follow our every move.

Flying on Talon's back, Roan and I are quiet. He seems to be deep in thought. Maybe he's trying to think of another approach, or other sources for the gemstone, if one exists. On the other hand, he could be angry that I won't be leaving him. What if he's done with me? He is male, after all, so it's possible that intimacy is what he'd hoped for and now that he's gotten it, he wants to dump me off at the nearest village or city.

Instead of going all the way back to Roan's cabin, Talon lands near a fast-flowing river, allowing us a break and herself refreshment. Sitting in the grass, staring at the water dancing along, we nibble on chunks of boar meat and drink from his satchel of water.

"I'm sorry," Roan says. "If anyone could have helped, it would have been them."

"It wasn't your fault," I reply. "It's human nature's fault. If people don't get what they want, the worst of us will just fight for it. Even if it apparently doesn't exist." The whole time we were flying, he didn't wish to be rid of me. Instead, guilt weighed heavily on his every thought.

He faces me, his eyes filled with longing. "Would you be content enough just to stay with me?"

Those words strike my chest, anxiety gripping tight. Home, so far away and impossible to reach. Memories overwhelm me, seeming so distant, like they are from another lifetime. Who do I have left there? I don't care about my house, my car, or money. I wouldn't need any of it here. All I have, aside from belongings, is one friend whom I consider family. I would hate to leave Katrina without the knowledge of my whereabouts, but what other options are there? Thoughts of staying here replace the memories of my past. Roan would protect me, look after me, and be with me. For so long I have dreamed of a place like this, so what am I so afraid of?

"Please," he says, "say something. I know it hasn't been long... and we have much to learn about each other... but I'm in love with you. If you still want to leave, I vow to do everything in my power to help you find a way home until my dying breath."

Tears escape my eyes, trickling down my cheek, and reaching my lips to leave a salty taste in my mouth. "You... love me?" Is it possible to fall in love so fast? Can you meet someone and know within two days that you want to spend the rest of your life with them?

Roan smiles and wipes a tear from my face. "I do."

With a deep breath, words form in my mind. However I respond, it must resemble precisely how I feel, so it's clear to him exactly what I want. "It is important that we don't give up on finding a way for any human to return home, if they so wish."

Roan's shoulders slowly slump and his gaze lowers.

"If you are willing to help me do this, then... I will stay with you."

He meets my gaze, eyes wide.

"Because... I love you, too." The craziness of it all is beyond overwhelming. How could I go through a secret and hidden portal to a strange world, meet an elf-guy and fall in love without even trying? Katrina would think I'm nuts.

Roan grabs me, pulling me into his arms, and we fall backward to roll around in the grass. Laughter escapes my lips as he tickles and teases me, while moisture from the ground soaks my clothes. A large huff sounds, and a spray of water saturates us both.

Together we sit upright to find Talon staring at us. She snorts, a damp mist leaving her nostrils, then she returns to fishing in the river. Roan and I laugh in response, and I wish there was a way I could get back at Talon for the thoughtful shower.

Roan kisses me long and hard.

A voice enters my thoughts. *I told you I had a plan,* Talon says. *From the moment you came to us, I sensed a connection between the two of you. Welcome to your new home, Tara of Earth. Welcome.*

The End

About the Authors

Sable BooKnight is proud to introduce you to the talented authors of Sable's first ever anthology, *Portals*. They hail from Saskatchewan, Manitoba and Illinois, each bringing their own unique voice and creativity. It would mean a great deal to these authors if you would take the time to leave an honest review on your preferred platform, or on Goodreads.

Denise Fenez

My name is Denise Fenez. I am a graduate of the University of Winnipeg 1995. I received a Bachelor of Arts Degree in English and Sociology at the age of 50. I then directed a mission called Anishinabe Fellowship Centre for the Presbyterian Church of Canada for 5 years. I turned 80 this year and was feeling depressed until my neighbour said, "I remember 80, that was 19 years ago.

This led to my decision to get busy and do something constructive; so I joined the Teulon Writers' group.

Eric McKinnon

Eric McKinnon has had numerous short stores published in editions of, Voices, Journal of the Lake Winnipeg Writers' Group. Born in Winnipeg, raised in Selkirk, he lived in Komarno for decades with his wife, Judy. They now live in Teulon.

Eric's short story,Peg,won the Lake Winnipeg Writers' Group's fiction writing contest of 2005; Coquette, was published in,From the Asylum Books and Press, a publication located in Dickinson, Texas, in 2006. His short story, The Snow Queen, placed first in the Short Story category of the 2010 Icelandic Festival (Islendingadagurinn) Writing Contest. He also placed in the Festival's 2010 Poetry Contest with a poem honouring his late grandfather, Kristjan Palsson, samples of whose poetry may be found in Interlake libraries.

He co-authored a collection of short stores in 2008 called, Don't Worry, it's Just the Wind... He published his first book of poetry, Weird Words, A Collection of Unusual Poetry, in 2018. He published his second book of poetry, Other Words, in 2023; his short story collection, Tales of the Uncanny & Mysterious, was published in 2025.

He is a founding member of the Teulon Library Writers' Group started in 2025.

Greg Shedden

Greg Shedden is a retired educator with over 30 years teaching experience at the grade 2 to grade 12 levels. He is proud to have been recognized as a Prime Minister's Teacher of Excellence, Provincial High School Teacher of the Year and Manitoba Council of International Cooperation Teacher of the Year.

Today Greg is a proud Grampa to a very special boy, father to two caring and hard-working young men and loving husband to a very generous and supportive wife. He enjoys working in his gardens, painting, writing in a variety of genres and is still active as a substitute teacher.

Lasalina Tess

Dreaming of other worlds, Lasalina Tess weaves her creative web through words, enveloping readers in exciting stories. Filled with magic and mystical creatures, Lasalina's stories take readers on epic adventures to her fantasy world of Calidora. Busy at her computer, she's working on high fantasy novels in this world, and is excited to share them with readers in the near future.

Find more about Lasalina at https://sablebooknight.ca/lasalina-tess/

Rebecca Hunnie

My name is Rebecca Hunnie, I was born the third child of four. Juggling early to find my place. It took a great loss in 2002 to help me find my love of writing. Being a single mother now has helped me become stronger as a person, writer and mother. I have battled multiple diagnoses from doctors and therapists and have come out stronger. Learning to grow as a writer has been a challenge I have loved to learn.

Sianyn Leigh

Fantasy author Sianyn Leigh grew up reading old fairy tales at her grandmother's knee, developing a passion for history, mythology, and the importance of storytelling. Inspired by the rich pantheons, folklore, and superstitions across the world, she enjoys exploring the "what ifs" of life's many questions and weaving them into fanciful tales.

After a decade in the indie publishing industry, Sianyn founded the independent press Chaos and Ink Books in 2024. She squeezes writing time and business operations around her day job in Medical Billing.

Sianyn resides in Central Illinois with her partner, son, and two energetic dogs.

T. Masters-Heinrichs

T. Masters-Heinrichs writes to entertain. She is a member of two serious writing groups and one for fun. Her short stories have appeared in: *Voices, Journal of the Lake Winnipeg Writers' Group*; *Interlake, Arts, Life and Leisure Magazine*; *Halloween Alliance* (http://halloweenalliance.com) and *Pages of Story* (http://www.pagesofstories.com).

Tania Stephanson

Tania Stephanson is an award-winning author best known for her crime thriller novel Red Crimes and non-fiction story Living Undiagnosed. She shares her knowledge of writing and publishing with other writers on her YouTube channel called Tania's Writing Realm. When she's not writing, Tania spends quality time with her two sons, husband and dog in Manitoba, Canada.

Discover more about Tania Stephanson, her publications and join her email list at https://sablebooknight.ca/tania-stephanson/

Stop by her Facebook page

https://www.facebook.com/TaniaStephanson

Trynda E. Adair

Trynda E. Adair grew up in Clandeboye, Manitoba, where she first shared stories among friends. Published since 2011, she continues to release short fiction and is currently developing several novel series. Alongside her writing, she works in web and software development and produces Gaelic-language publications, including the bi-monthly magazine *LUD*. Her creative work is shaped by a deep interest in Catholic and biblical theology, history, and language. When not writing or building digital tools, she can be found reading, researching, or exploring the intersection of faith, story, and culture.

Official Website: www.authortryndaadair.ca

Whitney R. Holp

Whitney R. Holp is a writer from Saskatchewan. He studied Journalism at the University of Regina and worked at various odd jobs while writing his first book. A surrealist, he seeks gnosis through dreams, intoxication, and objective chance. This story is from his forthcoming book *The Old Carter Place*.

Submit to Sable BooKnight!

Thank you for supporting Sable BooKnight authors!
The goal of Sable BooKnight's anthologies, is to bring writers together, and to help them reach new readers. If you are interested in submitting to one of Sable's future anthologies, visit https://sablebooknight.ca/submissions for information on upcoming projects. Please read the detailed submission guidelines prior to submission.

www.ingramcontent.com/pod-product-compliance
Lightning Source LLC
LaVergne TN
LVHW020714110826
845149LV00012B/2254
9781990282409